P9-DDG-398

Brandywine Hundred Library
1300 Foulk Rd.
Wilmington, DE 19803

THE BISCUIT WITCH

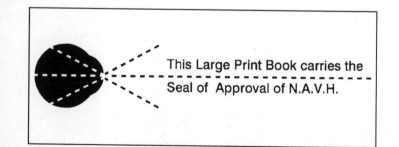

This Large Print Book carries the
Seal of Approval of N.A.V.H.

THE MACBRIDES

THE BISCUIT WITCH

A CROSSROADS CAFÉ NOVELLA

DEBORAH SMITH

THORNDIKE PRESS

A part of Gale, Cengage Learning

GALE
CENGAGE Learning·

Farmington Hills, Mich • San Francisco • New York • Waterville, Maine
Meriden, Conn • Mason, Ohio • Chicago

GALE
CENGAGE Learning®

Copyright © 2013 by Deborah Smith.
Thorndike Press, a part of Gale, Cengage Learning.

ALL RIGHTS RESERVED
This is a work of fiction. Names, characters, places, and incidents are either the products of the author's imagination or are used fictitiously. Any resemblance to actual persons (living or dead), events or locales is entirely coincidental.
Thorndike Press® Large Print Clean Reads.
The text of this Large Print edition is unabridged.
Other aspects of the book may vary from the original edition.
Set in 16 pt. Plantin.

LIBRARY OF CONGRESS CATALOGING-IN-PUBLICATION DATA

Smith, Deborah, 1955–
    The Biscuit Witch : a Crossroads Café novella / by Deborah Smith. — Large Print edition.
      pages cm. — (Thorndike Press Large Print Clean Reads) (The MacBrides ; Book 1)
    ISBN-13: 978-1-4104-6818-5 (hardcover)
    ISBN-10: 1-4104-6818-6 (hardcover)
    1. Life change events—Fiction. 2. Homecoming—Fiction. 3. Coffee shops—Fiction. 4. Biscuits—Fiction. 5. Appalachian Region—Fiction. 6. North Carolina—Fiction. 7. Large type books. I. Title.
PS3569.M5177B57 2014
813'.54—dc23
                                      2013050884

Published in 2014 by arrangement with BelleBooks, Inc.

Printed in Mexico
1 2 3 4 5 6 7 18 17 16 15 14

A RAMBLING DEDICATION
AND THEN SOME

My mother has been gone for six years now, and I find that the piece of my heart that will always belong to her wants to be a mama, just as she was. It's the only way I can share the mystical realm of mamahood with her. I know she's up there in Mama Land, watching me from an old kitchen chair in front of a screened window filled with sunlight and the scent of fresh mowed grass. She has a smoke in one hand and a glass of vodka in the other. Her favorite lap dog, Burford the Killer Miniature Schnauzer, is growling at the mailman outside. An episode of *Matlock* has just ended on the TV, and *Golden Girls* is about to start. She checks in on me during the commercials.

This morning she knocked one of my candle sconces off the wall in the kitchen entry. They're her sconces; actually, I just inherited them for safe-keeping. She uses them as her go-to signal. I'm never quite sure what she's trying to tell me, but whenever a sconce falls off its nails I stop and listen hard.

Whazzup, Ma?

She knew I'd be writing this dedication for *The Biscuit Witch* today. I'm telling you about her and Mama Land because that sconce fell off. I think this was her goal.

I am trying my best to carry on her Mama traditions. I've decided it's my duty to find young people within the age groups of the children I might have had, and to pester them. To dote on them, give them advice whether they want it or not, worry about their decisions, cheer their victories, and remind them that they are unique, glorious, grand and special.

"Team Awesome" is what we call Brittany Shirley, Danielle Childers, and Jenny Mc-Knatt at the offices of Bell Bridge Books. All three are smarter than I ever was at their ages, also prettier, funnier, and more mature (in fact they're more mature than I am now.)

The world is safe in their hands. The future

is bright. If I could go back in time and pick out the best of the litter to be a mama to, I'd pick them.

And so this book is dedicated to them and to all of us, the daughters (and sons) of Mama Land.

I'll go put that wall sconce back into place. I hear you, Ma. I miss you.

This book would not exist without the arm-twisting, cheerleading, ever-patient leadership of my sister-of-the-heart, Debra Dixon, the best editor I've ever had, bar none, and the yarn mentor who got me addicted to knitting and crochet, which is why people run from me when they see me coming with more scarves to give away. Nor would it exist without co-sister Pam Ireland, aka SHE WHO WRITES THE CHECKS, also known as THE DOG WHISPERER. She has tried her best to counsel me as a Dog Mama, and it's not her fault that my furry children are obese, lazy, impolite and play way too many video games.

Last and never least, without my Hubby, Hank, there would be nothing. No books, no celebration, no serenity, and probably no Me. My shadow would lurk in corners, try-

7

ing to reprogram the TV remote, reset the default on the smart phone's ringtone, and make the laptop stop beeping. Many electronics would suffer. There would be no homemade veggie stew, no bills paid on time, no ebooks designed, no batteries jumped, no bed warmed, and no one to yell, "What the dang was THAT about?" during *Game of Thrones, True Blood,* and *Pawn Stars.* There would be no soulmate, and no soul. Just me in a house filled with broken machines. I would adopt dozens of cats, dogs, goats, rabbits, ferrets, parakeets and chickens. Also miniature donkeys and full-sized ducks. I would fill the windows with colored glass bottles and answer the door carrying a shotgun while wearing a house-dress with "Blessed are the Cracked, for they let in the Light," hand-lettered across the bosom in food coloring.

It would be sad. And smelly.

I'm so glad I have him, and DD and Pam and Team Awesome and all our mutual friends to keep me out of that housedress. This one's for you all, y'all. With love.

"Of course there's magic in food! It's the lure of our hopes and dreams. A good meal can make people smile, forget their sorrows, remember their friends, and fall in love. That's why we take food to funerals. To remember how good it tastes to be alive."

— The late biscuit witch, Jane Eve Nettie MacBride, mother of Tal, Gabby and Gus, great grand-niece of the infamous biscuit witch, Mary Eve Nettie, and close cousin to the famous biscuit witch, Delta Whittlespoon of The Crossroads Café

PROLOGUE

Delta Rescues Another Lost and Hungry Soul

Dear Doctor Firth,

I run my kitchen and my life by two sayings: *Good food speaks louder than words,* and *Nobody's a stranger, just a cousin waiting to be recognized.*

Maybe that second one is a southern idea, even more than most. Howsomeever, here goes.

I read about you at Whittlespoons R Us, the online genealogy newsletter for my husband's (Sheriff Pike Whittlespoon of Jefferson County, North Carolina) family. Your great-grandfather Angus Firth of Glasgow is Pike's third cousin twice removed on his daddy's side, through the Jefferson line, meaning it's likely that you share the Jefferson appreciation for cloven-hooved animals, liquor, family, good food, and the other passions of living. (Sex! Football!)

I know you are in your cups at this time, drinking, taking pills, and sleeping under trees, but I have some experience rehabilitating lost souls in that regard, and so I am enclosing a box of my biscuits and a cold-wrapped container of cream gravy for dessert. Please eat and write back.

We need a veterinarian of your gumption here in the Crossroads Cove of Jefferson County. My famous movie-star cousin, Cathy Deen Mitternich, and her husband, Thomas, have purchased assorted goats for their estate on Wild Woman Ridge, and our local berry farmers and lesbians, Alberta and Macy Spruill-Groover, wish to add sheep to their collection of critters and abused women they shelter. We could use an animal doctor who doesn't mind progressive Oddness.

If you are willing to move up here, I have Jay Wakefield's permission to offer you a no-rent fixer-upper on his property at the nearby haunted village of Free Wheeler. Since Jay has become a friend of yours already, you know he is one of the richer-than-Midas-and-stingierthan-Scrooge Wakefields of Asheville, but did you know this? He's related to me on his grandmother's father's side, so he's got a soft heart for peculiarities. I've been dosing him with biscuits and gravy since he was a bitter teenager stuck in a private boarding school, and I believe I've greased his view of the Wakefield family curse.

I can also promise you plenty of friendship among the local women plus Saturday night card games at Pike's poker trailer, free meals at the Crossroads Café, and enough veterinary business to build yourself a decent income here in the Cove (and also over at Turtleville, our county seat). Most of all, I promise you lots of biscuits.

Come home, Cousin Douglas Firth of Scotland and now from Florida. You know we are descended from the same stock, don't you? Mountaineering Irish and Scots and Scots-Irish around here? Plus Cherokee, African American, Vikings, outcast Romans, the Ten Tribes of Israel, and space aliens (That last one is harder to prove.)

You'll fit right in.

Love,
Cousin Delta.

Doug, Three Years Later

A Scotsman, two lesbians, an agoraphobic knitter, five herding dogs, and three hundred sheep walk into a bar and . . .

Ought to make a fine joke, you'd think. But it was for real, that is, the reality as I've come to know and love it, another day in the gently accepting world o' the Cove, or, in this case, one mile *higher* than the Cove in altitude, up on the ridges of the Little Sheba, one of the Ten Sisters Mountains.

Damn sheep don't need to go to pasture up here. Lots o' fine pastureland down in the Cove. That's what I get for hiring Alberta and Macy Spruill-Groover to tend my herd along with theirs. Lesbian feminist shepherds!

"The feminine urge to explore should be nurtured," they said.

"The instincts of the ewes come from the Mother Goddess," they said. "The Mother Goddess says they must follow the call to roam."

Then I say Mother Goddess could come up here *by herself* in the arse-chilling November cold and risk being run over by a speeding poultry truck or a pack of joy-riding bikers. We were herding the sheep down the Asheville Trace. Even at its best, the narrow old two-lane is a steep, winding launch ramp for idiots on wheels. We'd have taken an off-road route instead, but the temperature was dropping fast. Had to get home before the fall lambs froze to their mams' teats.

"Trouble ahead, Doc!" Macy shouted. Alberta started whistling commands to the sheep dogs. I was bringing up the rear, trying not to step in sheep dung, at least not before my new hiking boots got the shine of the Turtleville Shoe Bee Hiking Store rubbed off. Macy and Alberta were hidden around a curve at the front of the flock. Lucy Parmenter looked back at me from her seat atop a tractor, her face going so pale she could be one of my grandmama's blond ceramic dolls back in Glasgow. *Before* Grandmama painted their bisque-white faces.

"No worries, Luce, just hold the course," I soothed. She nodded shakily then faced forward. For Lucy Parmenter to creep out of her fiber studio at Rainbow Goddess Farm was a huge step forward; driving this tractor pulling a wagon full of lambs was an accomplishment that made Macy, her therapist, dance a jig.

"No dawdling," I growled, as the ewes ahead of me began to slow or even stop. Sheep are the lookie-loo's of the herd world.

Give them any distraction whatsoever, and they'll cause a traffic jam. You'd have better luck making good time on a city highway during rush hour behind a stalled bus full of naked strippers giving away free Lotto tickets.

Lots of insulting *bahs* came my way, and the ripple of slow/stop behavior continued to build. Around the curve, the dogs began to bark, and Alberta stopped whistling and started yelling. "Down. Stay. *No!*"

"What in the hell is going on up there?" I muttered. Propping my walking stick on one shoulder, I strode through the flock as fast as I could.

"Tagger's finally caught a car!" Macy yelled.

A cranky veterinarian, two lesbian goddess worshipers, a little blond fiber artist who's about to faint like a frightened bunny, a stalled herd of sheep, five freaked-out Belgian Sheepdogs, and a giant black bear named Tagger walk into a bar . . .

. . . and I meet Tal MacBride.

CHAPTER ONE

Tallulah MacBride, The Biscuit Witch

When Mama died, I heard her heart stop beating. And then, she spoke to me.

My head was burrowed on her chest as she lay on the cold linoleum floor of our little house in West Asheville. I was six years old. Her heart thumped in my ear in rhythm to my sobs. Around me I heard Gabby ordering "Mama, breathe!" and Gus yelling our address into the kitchen phone.

But I shut them out so I could concentrate on the softening, slowing, hesitating beat of Mama's heart. When the sound faded away to nothing, a terrifying stillness rose up inside me. Some people believe a person's spirit lingers for a while after the body stops living, but not me. The silent darkness of her stopped heart opened like a black well, and I fell in. I can't describe the infinite emptiness of that moment when the sweet thump of her heart ended, that infinity between one heart beat to the silence of forever. I can only say I tried to follow the trail of silence. Tried to follow Mama wherever she'd gone.

I want to go with you. Anywhere. There must be an Anywhere if you're going there.

Except for what happened next, I might not have survived that plunge. I would have left some important part of my soul behind in the unleavened silence of a dark, distant heaven.

The aroma of apple pie suddenly surrounded me. Not the pie Mama had splattered on the floor when she fell, but the soul of it, Mama's soul, just like the angel I'd seen floating in the steam above the stove a few minutes before she collapsed.

Mama had gone with that pie angel.

She whispered to me.

Gus and Gabby need you, baby. You're the only one who can take care of them for me. Go on back now, you hear? And keep them safe. You're the biscuit witch. Gabby's the pickle queen, and Gus is the kitchen charmer.

I still can't describe the wonder of that whisper. Even in the deepest grief, I knew I had a job to do. Somehow, I — the baby of the family — would become the quirky starch that held us together.

I promise. I will. But oh, Mama. Don't go.

I have to, baby. But I'll always be here when you cook for love.

Small children can hear the whispers of angels. The nature of unleavened childhood is so open to magic and so quiet. We are born inside our mothers, listening to their heartbeats, surrounded by their life. That memory never dies.

I heard. I believed.

Tal Remembers . . . Baked, Pickled and Stewed

Family scandals are like most "secret" family recipes — not very secret and not that special. Their mystique comes from the fact that, once upon a time, someone cared enough to hide them. Our grandmother, Emma Nettie, proved that a really good cook can dish up a scandal worthy of the name. Its secret ingredient? Our grandfather.

No one knew his identity. Not even Mama. Grandma Emma died in nineteen fifty-two when Mama was still a baby. Nettie's relatives raised Mama. Had Grandma Emma been a shameful trollop or just a free spirit? A bootlegger's babe or a minister's girlfriend? Or both?

The known ingredients were these: she was a half-sister to Mary Eve Nettie, the

Wild Woman of Wild Woman Ridge, high in the Ten Sisters Mountains northwest of Asheville. Mary Eve was no shrinking violet either but managed to establish a more conventional brand of free-thinking woman-hood than Emma. Both were great cooks.

Biscuit witches, Mama called them. She'd heard the term as a girl. She'd inherited that talent. My mother, Jane Eve Nettie MacBride, could cast spells on total strangers simply by setting a plate of her biscuits in front of them.

Mary Eve taught both Mama and her cousin, Delta Whittlespoon, to cook. Mama and Delta ran together as teens, working as short-order cooks and waitresses, smoking inventive substances, sipping homemade wine, chugging cheap beer, and sampling illegal corn whiskey (moonshine that's been aged to mellow it). Mama was twenty-two when Mary Eve died. Delta was twenty.

Delta married Pike Whittlespoon, the future sheriff of Jefferson County, and Mama married our heroic Daddy, Stewart MacBride — farm boy, ex-army sarge, and Asheville police officer. She and Daddy scraped together the money for her to open Baked, Pickled and Stewed, the best hole-in-the-wall diner in Asheville, down the hill on Lexington Avenue, which was not the fine bohemian boulevard of hippies, slackers, art students, mimes, musicians, and tourist traffic it is today, but was then a place of forgotten storefronts and boarded-over vintage office buildings, where even the once glam Victorian gargoyles looked worried about the neighborhood.

Daddy built the diner's tables out of rescued shipping pallets, and the chairs were salvaged from a tobacco warehouse that had been converted to a used furniture store out near Weaverville. Thus, the Baked, Pickled and Stewed Diner had everything from cane-backed chairs to sixties' vinyl, seventies' Naugahhyde, church pews, and a long hand-carved bench with toilet holes spaced along it. (Mama covered them with an upholstered plank.) Somewhere, a community outhouse was missing its sing-along room.)

Before long, the B, P and S became the must-go eatery for breakfast, lunch, and take-out dinners in the go-go years of the nineteen seventies. (Closing at seven p.m. every night so Mama could spend evenings with us and Daddy.) Mama believed in "farm-to-table" freshness decades before the marketing weasels coined that term. She offered herb-seasoned home cooking and from-scratch baking, plus sold her canned

21

jellies, jams, relishes, and MacBride secret-recipe pickles. Daddy washed dishes and bussed tables, prepped vegetables, and kept the accounts.

Within the first two years, she and Daddy made enough money for a down payment on a house over in West Asheville — the bad side of town, putting it politely. Drive west out of the city, down Chicken Hill through the old cotton mill district, past the abandoned turn-of-the-century buildings of the river district, over the bridge at the French Broad, and up into a woodsy community of small clapboard homes and run-down shops built in the twenties and thirties. West Asheville had never quite recovered from the Depression forty years earlier.

Mama and Daddy didn't mind the shabby surroundings. They were proud owners of a three-bedroom bungalow with a porch, two acres of yard, a clearing just perfect for a garden, and lots of play space for kids.

When Gus was born, Daddy revealed what would, in today's terms, be called his "metrosexual streak." Our big, freckled, ass-kicking, deer-hunting, red-headed Daddy loved old Hollywood movies the way crows love cornfields and shiny cans. Thus, our brother was christened Groucho Marx MacBride. Four years later, when our sister was born, he wanted to name her "Harpo." At which point Mama donned her pink Jellies (it was the nineteen eighties, after all) and put her foot down. So Daddy compromised, and my sister was christened Greta Garbo MacBride.

Two years after that, I came along. Daddy conceded again or else my name might be Chico.

Instead, I am Tallulah Bankhead MacBride.

The three of us roamed the empty lots and kudzu-tangled woods of our forgotten neighborhood like fearless explorers. Gus and Gabby cleared a trail from our backyard down to the French Broad River, where Gus built a cook pit from river rocks, Gabby dug up interesting roots to boil, and I tamed squirrels by offering them treats: my Little Miss Baking Oven cookies, which would have tasted better if the oven were powered by something hotter than a sixty-watt light bulb. I am living proof: raw cookie dough will not kill a determined junior chef.

Our childhoods were a sunny, buttery-good paradise until Daddy got killed rescuing a family from a backroads wreck. A tractor-trailer swung loose on the icy mountain road and sideswiped him. Mama broke into little pieces, though she put up a brave front for our sakes. The diner suffered, and the landlord — who owned big chunks of Asheville and wanted to tear down every building older than a well-aged brie — cancelled her lease.

She took a job on the factory line at a potato-chip company, collapsed in our kitchen one night two months later, and died before the ambulance came. The doctors called it an aneurysm, but the truth was this: Mama died of betrayal and a broken heart. She was only thirty-nine years old.

Gus was eleven. Gabby was nine, and I was six. Delta fought to adopt us, but the paperwork fell through because of a bungled file at the courthouse. We escaped from foster care with the help of an elderly neighbor who sent us to California to live with friends who operated several restaurants in Los Angeles. The Rodriquez's were older and had only one child, a daughter who proved to be Gus's undoing eventually. Plus they had a soft spot for illegal immigrants. That's how our status felt. We laid low, grew up, and never forgot the pain of being outcasts.

Delta loved us from afar all that time, sending food and encouragement.

We had never forgotten that.

She was proof that family recipes, even the secret ones, are worth keeping. Even if they come to us on tattered paper with tears and stains and missing ingredients.

Tal's Biscuit Wishes and Unread Mail

We were raised to minister to the hungry, to nourish the sorrowful and bear witness to the fruitful joys of shared food, but somehow our lives had become a messy buffet of half-baked dreams, sour hopes, and bitter brews. Mama and Daddy trained us to stay true to our inner appetites, but we lost our *whey.* If life is a menu, our Daily Specials should be sent back to the kitchen for a second try. As mountain cooks say: *If you can't stand the heat, go lick a different pepper.*

Find a wall, smack my head against it, and think about my life so far. That was *my* motto at the moment.

I was running from Eve's father, thanks to an arrest warrant that had been issued after he said I assaulted him with a cupcake decoration. I'd do whatever it took to protect Eve, especially from the man who fathered her. Mark Anthony Mark, New York's most famous restaurant entrepreneur, the star of the top-rated 'Mark Anthony Mark's *Cuisine!*' on the extremely popular Kitchen TV Network, didn't want to be part of her life. He just wanted to make certain no one found out he'd never wanted her at all.

"Oy! You've got another card from that peculiar cousin of yours," my Brooklyn landlord, Mirielle, reported. "The envelope smells like . . . like milk and sausage. Puh-tooey! Do you want me to open it?"

A birthday card from Delta. She never missed our birthdays.

"No, just save it with the rest of the mail, thank you."

Talking to Mirielle Steinburg was the last conversation I risked before I wrapped my cell phone in foil inside a cookie tin so no one could track me using its GPS. I was driving out of New York when she called, with Eve napping in the back seat of my Bronco.

"You and Eve will return soon?" Mirielle asked.

"Yes, in four or five days."

"I hope it's worth it to drive all the way to Minnesota to buy an oven for the shop!"

I had no idea where we were going. The Minnesota story was a cover. "It's a good deal I can't pass up. Bye, and thanks again for collecting my mail. I'll read Delta's card when I get back!"

I stuffed the phone inside a wad of tin foil

and then into the small cookie tin. I'd researched this on the web. Mark's hired snoops couldn't track my phone signals.

Plan. I needed a plan. California, with Gabby, was too far away. Where else . . .

Delta.

That's it! I'd take Eve to North Carolina and ask Delta to hide us. Delta would give us sanctuary. The Cousinhood of the Biscuit Witches is a powerful bond.

I'd go home.

Home?

North Carolina? We hadn't been back in over twenty years. My *home* was a tiny two-room walk-up in Brooklyn, above my cupcake bakery. I saw the cake pan as half-full, never half-empty. Everyone thought I was too soft in the middle, too sweet around the edges, and I needed a thicker crust. Gus was stout-hearted. Gabby was salty, and I kneaded to be needed.

What did home mean to me, Gus, and Gabby now? After fifteen years in the army, four tours of the Middle East, and a chest full of medals, Captain Gus MacBride still volunteered for duty in the most dangerous parts of Afghanistan. He had an open-ended offer to return stateside as a training instructor at Fort Merrill, the ranger camp down in Georgia, but he kept stalling. We begged him to see that he'd done what he promised to do when Daddy died — be the man of the family, take care of Mama and us. We knew he'd used up all his luck with too many close calls. Gabby and I were terrified that he'd come home in a coffin.

Out in Los Angeles, Gabby, thirty-one, was about to lose everything she thought she'd ever wanted: her Porsche, her expensive townhouse in a suburb of Long Beach, and her restaurant, in a court battle with her high-maintenance movie-star partner, John Michael Michael.

Obviously, she and I shared an affinity for men with odd names.

What would I find in the mountains? Maybe just a reason to leave again. Julia Child said this about cooking, but it applies to life, too: "You've got to have a 'what-the-hell' attitude."

It's not just what you remember that leads you back home. It's what you don't want to forget.

One Day Later . . .
How Tagger Caught Tal, Eve, and a Cupcake
"Mommy, are we driving through a zoo?" Eve asked from the back seat of our ancient SUV. I'd pulled off on the roadside to study

28

a map again. The old-fashioned, fold-out, paper kind.

Our meandering route was named the Asheville Trace — an aged, graying two-lane with a faded center line and crumbling edges. Winter trees crowded close on one side. On the other, rivulets of ice marked the paths of water trickling down a craggy wall of rock. At a distant curve, the alley of rock and trees opened to reveal a soaring view of rounded mountaintops sinking into an ocean of silver clouds. Somewhere in the vast view of forest, mountain peaks, and the occasional small river was the Crossroads Cove. We'd left Asheville two hours ago, but still, no sign of the Cove. The bright blue post-Thanksgiving November sky had gone cloudy with the last survivors of brilliant red and gold leaves whisking across the windshield. The weather report at our Asheville motel had promised freezing temps by nightfall.

"No, sweetie, we're not in a zoo or a wild animal park or anything," I told Eve. "Why do you think so?" I tugged off a wide, knitted headband — deep purple with multi-colored pom poms, because Eve picked it out for my birthday at a Brooklyn thrift shop, and the dancing bobbles on my head made her laugh. Warm air gushed from the

SUV's untrustworthy heater, which had two settings: Shiver and Sweat. I dabbed my forehead with the headband. I hadn't slept well in weeks. Shanks of long, tangled red hair fell on either side of my face. I had no peripheral vision, or I would have shrieked.

"A bear is licking my window," Eve said calmly.

I pivoted in the driver's seat. Sure enough, a huge black bear was placidly licking the passenger-side back window, inches from my red-haired princesses' curious face. She touched the spot where its long pink tongue hit the glass. "Hello, Mr. Bear! Would you like a Monkey Poop cupcake?" She unbuckled her seatbelt and turned to fetch a cupcake from a container next to her. On the drive down from New York I'd distracted her by baking her favorite — a banana-flavored cake mix topped with banana-flavored yellow frosting. Thus, the name, Monkey Poop. A desk clerk let me use the kitchen of the motel's complimentary breakfast alcove.

"No!" I hit the automatic door locks. "No, sweetie, we can't open the window and feed Mr. Bear. He might accidentally nibble us. Just sit tight. We're leaving."

"But he looks hungry, Mommy. And cold." Her green eyes, like mine — and

Gabby's, and Gus's. We inherited them from Daddy — were shadowed and tired. No matter how many times I told her we were on a vacation trip to meet our North Carolina relatives, she sensed that all was not well. For one thing, I'd never pulled her out of kindergarten in mid-week before. School was very important. She planned to be an astronaut, a doctor, or a toll booth collector. "Mr. Bear looks sad and worried," she said in a small voice. "He's like me. He needs a Monkey Poop to cheer him up."

I caved. "All right, I'll drive up the road a little ways then stop and throw a cupcake out. Wave bye-bye to the bear. We'll sit in the car and watch him eat."

She brightened. "Okay."

I turned the ignition key. *Clatter, clang, rattle rattle, brrrrrr.* Then silence. I groaned. Two dead batteries in three years. Three, counting this one. "Aw, dammit!"

"Aw, dammit," Eve repeated solemnly.

The bear acted as if he understood the situation. Now, we were at his mercy. He thrust his snout against a wide patch of duct tape I'd plastered over the top third of the passenger window. The window sometimes refused to roll all the way down, or, conversely, to roll all the way back up. I was still a southerner at heart. Give us some

31

duct tape and baling wire, and we can fix anything.

The duct tape surged inward, tented by Mr. Bear's large nose. I unbuckled, climbed over the center console, and slapped the imprint it made. He snorted, shook his huge head, and poked the tape again. I rapped the bulge with my knuckles. "Go! Get back! Beat it!"

He sneezed then shoved harder. The patch started ripping away from the door frame. I grabbed my faux-leather tote off the floor, pulled out a hairbrush, and repeatedly whacked the bulge that continued to get bigger and protrude further inside the car.

"Here, Mommy, he just wants a cupcake." Eve leaned between the seats and held one toward the bulge.

"Sweetie, sit down!"

I pushed her backwards and grabbed the cupcake from her. The Bronco rocked as the bear plowed his big chest and shoulders into its side. The window patch ripped away.

Suddenly I was nose-to-nose with *his* nose and his lapping tongue. Both of his round, black ears were adorned with several metal tags. Not a good sign. He had a criminal record. A repeat offender. I glimpsed white fangs big enough to punch holes in steel siding. A whoosh of cold air rushed inside along with the greasy stink of unwashed ursine funk. The bear wrapped his tongue around my hand *and* the cupcake. I let go, and the cupcake disappeared into his toothy maw. Chomp, chomp, swallow.

I jerked my slobber-covered hand away and scrambled between the seats into the back. My knees sank into something gushy. The open plastic container full of Monkey Poop cupcakes.

He shoved again. The window buckled. A sound like popcorn popping filled my ears as the safety glass cracked. "Cover your face and get down!" I yelled to Eve. The window collapsed. I pushed her to the floor. Pebbles of glass bounced merrily. The bear shoved his entire head and neck into the Bronco, sniffing avidly. The Bronco was *full* of bear. He was practically sitting in the passenger seat.

Eve, my amazing child, was giggling like crazy. I turned myself into a human shield, sitting in the center of the back seat and shielding her body by jamming my knees into the opening between the front seats. I glared at the bear. I became Sigourney Weaver facing the giant bug-like creature in *Alien*.

Get away from her, you bastard.

But unlike Sigourney, the front of my legs

33

was covered in banana-flavored cake mix and yellow icing.

The bear sniffed hard at me and uttered a soft, hungry noise. *"Mawr."*

"He wants more," Eve translated.

Slurp. Who knew bears have such long, stretchable tongues? His snout hovered over the center console. My cupcake-smeared knees were easily reached. He began licking me.

"Eve, sweetie, I want you to crawl over the seat into the cargo section, okay?"

"I wanna see what he's doing."

"You can watch from the back. Now go!"

She hustled over the seat and into the cargo area, chortling. "He's eating Monkey Poop off your blue jeans!"

Slurp. He was, indeed.

"I'm going to sit still, *very* still, until he finishes. He can't reach any farther inside the car. Black bears don't want to hurt people. He's just hungry. When your aunt and uncle and I were growing up outside Asheville, we saw bears all the time. We'll be fine."

He'd wander off. I'd clean up, dig out my cell phone even though I shouldn't, and call for help. No one in the Cove would ever know that Tallulah MacBride was not a bonafide North Carolinian anymore, but

34

instead, a New York City woman so damn clueless she got herself and her little girl trapped in the back of a decrepit SUV with a bear licking banana cupcake off her legs.

"Look, Mommy, somebody's coming," Eve said.

The road behind us was now full of four-footed spectators with dreadlocks. Sheep. Big sheep with long, corkscrew curls and dusky blue faces. Also, huge, shaggy black dogs. Two sturdy women were heading toward my Bronco, swooshing the air with shepherd's crooks straight out of *Little Bo Peep*. Unlike Miss Peep, they wore quilted coats over baggy overalls. Rainbow-hued knit caps covered curly red hair on one, long blond braids on the other.

Mr. Bear, still using me as a cupcake-delivery device, did not seem to care or notice.

"Tagger, you sneaky bastard!" the brawnier of the two women bellowed. "Get your freaking head out of that freaking window!"

"What's a 'freaking head,' Mommy?"

This was no time for a lecture on bad language. "The lady is just mad at Mr. Bear's head," I said. "Shhh."

That was no lady, that was ex-marine Alberta Spruill-Groover, who eschewed the term "lady" as a label meant to divide women into camps: Demure vs. Alberta. I would learn that later, during introductions. At the moment, I watched her smack the bear's large black rump with her crook.

"My Gawd," Alberta bawled through the windows. "What's in that goo on your knees? Bear bait? He's never done anything *this* ballsy before!"

Not only did the bear ignore her, he strained forward to lick my cupcake-coated self more efficiently. Alberta bent down further to peer at us through the back window. "Tagger's harmless," she said loudly. "See all those tags on his ears? He's been caught raiding campsites so many times the forestry service quit bothering to keep records. But *you* should know better. Don't feed the bears! This is not some kind of cutesy pie exhibit at Disneyland!"

"I didn't feed the bear. He broke in and fed himself."

"Why didn't you drive off?"

"Dead battery."

"Why didn't you just sit tight and wait for somebody to come by and give you a jump start? Why'd you open a window?"

"I didn't," I said through gritted teeth. "He opened it with his head."

"City girl, aren't you? This is why everybody oughta carry a gun. All you have to do is wave a gun at Tagger. He hates them."

"I have a nine millimeter Glock 19 in my tote." A gift from Gus. He gave Gabby one, also. There. My bonafides. Bite me, NRA spokeswoman.

"A gun doesn't do any damn good unless you get it out of your purse, girly."

Eve defended me. "Mommy wouldn't shoot Mr. Bear! So she got out her hair-brush and smacked him on the nose!"

Alberta stared at me. Her flat little lips formed an upside-down half-moon, the kind that precedes a snarky laugh and a full-blown eye-rolling. "You got a license to carry a lethal weapon like that?"

Okay, okay, my humiliation is complete.

She returned to whacking Tagger. Tagger continued to lick my legs.

Someone knocked on the opposite window. I swiveled quickly.

Looking at us was a lumberjack. Plaid flannel, canvas cargo pants, a fleece-lined jacket. Thick, wavy hair the rust-brown color of old copper shagged around his face. He had blue eyes under *Magnum P.I.*-era, Tom Selleck brows. His eyes were sad, even a little hard. Though he was bent over to look at us, he seemed very tall. He tapped a large knuckle on the window again.

When I frowned at him, he tilted his head and studied me, frowning in return.

"No worries, girls," he said in a deep Scottish brogue. He pivoted to look at Eve in the cargo bay. He touched a fingertip to the reflection of her wonder-filled eyes, and he smiled when she smiled back. It was like a sip of Scotch whiskey with a cinnamon bun for dessert. He lit up the car, the mountains, the universe.

He returned to frowning at me and tapped the window again, then pointed to his right ear. "Can you hear me?" he said loudly. "Do you have a wee bit of an ear problem?"

I pressed the window control. As it rolled down, the wind brought his scent to me. Flannel and wool and all man. "No, I have a wee bit of a *bear* problem."

"That's an interestin' way you have of dealin' with it."

"Food is a universal language. This bear and I are communicating through cupcakes. Is it safe to take my daughter out of the car?"

"Probably, but if you'll scrape some of that frosting back into its dish, I'll lure Tagger away with it first."

"It's called Monkey Poop," Eve told him, her voice low and distracted. She clasped the back seat and leaned over it, studying him fervently. I wondered what was churning in her five-year-old brain.

"Is it, sweetheart? The two of you are no' so good as bear bait, though you do smell like the sweetest bakery ever."

I felt heat rising in my face. I have freckles. They would now merge into a reddish pattern, and I'd resemble a half-ripe strawberry. I turned to the humiliating business of scraping banana cupcake goo off my jeans. Tagger never stopped licking me. To hell with it. I shoved his toothy snout aside and scooped the debris of six cupcakes into the plastic container.

"Good girl," the Scotsman said, having no apparent concern that "girl" is not the politically correct term for a twenty-nine-year-old bakery chef, mother, and human strawberry.

I handed him the container. "My name is Tal MacBride. And this is my daughter, Eve."

His mouth quirked. "The name's Doug Firth. A pleasure to meet you."

"We're lost," Eve put in. "And homeless."

"No, no," I corrected too quickly. "Lost, yes. Homeless, no."

"But Mommy, you said we can't go back home . . ."

"Could you tell me if the Crossroads Café

is far from here, Mr. Firth?"

He was studying us intently, those thick, young Selleck brows knitted together. *Time for a mommy-daughter talk about not repeating things Mommy says.*

His brows lifted. Good. Maybe he wouldn't pry. "Just down the mountain." He pointed ahead. "Keep going, and you can't miss it. The scent of biscuits will draw you right to the front door."

"Thank you."

"Doc!" Alberta Spruill-Groover hollered from behind us somewhere. "Bunny's gone belly up! Macy's going to drive the tractor the rest of the way."

"Can Bunny hop?" he called back.

"Nope. She's not good for even a single hippity."

He bent to me again. "One of our friends isn't feeling well. Could you give her a lift to yon café? It's just down the mountain a wee mile or two."

"We can do that. Okay. But first, can you give me a jump start?" That didn't come out right. I knew it, and so did he.

"My pleasure," he said. He put just enough English on our Cue Ball of Innuendo. It curved in a slow, sensuous arc and dropped deep into my corner pocket. I arched a warning brow. At the same time, my strawberry turned ripe for the picking.

"Doc? Can the Hairbrush Commando take Bunny in her Bearmobile?"

He sighed, straightened, and called back, "Aye, I've already asked her. Just let me jump her off, first."

Alberta's raucous hoots hit me like verbal paint balls. "We'll help Bunny wobble up there as soon as Tagger scrams."

"Give me five minutes, and Tagger will be on his way." Doc Firth stepped back, ducked his head at me, and smiled. "Thank you, girls . . . ladies . . . Tal and Eve."

Eve called out, "Mr. Bear won't eat you, will he?"

"No, sweetie, he's a gentleman. Give a little, get a little. Share the sweetness. The fellowship of food is not for us two-legged beasties alone." He walked around the front of the SUV, holding out the container of smushed cupcakes. Moving slowly and carefully, he leaned over the hood and waggled it. Tagger looked at him through my windshield, sniffed, then withdrew his head from my ruined window. He headed toward Doug.

"Watch out, Doc," Alberta warned. "Whatever that shit is, he seems to love it. He might lunge at you."

Doug Firth backed away slowly, calling

softly in his brogue, "Come along, beastie, come along." The giant bear lumbered after him like a big dog. I held my breath.

"I want to take Tagger home with us," Eve said. She looked at me sadly. "Where is our home? Is it really gone?"

"Our home is right here." I liked New York, but my roots were in these mountains. I touched a finger to her chest then to mine. She had been born inside me. She knew the sound of my heart. "Heart to heart."

"Look!" She pointed to the floor board. I retrieved an intact Monkey Poop cupcake. It was completely unharmed. Not a dent in the icing, not a single, slurpy slime-trail from Tagger's tongue, nothing. Eve sighed. "It's magic."

I watched Doug Firth stop at the edge of the woods. He held out my plastic container to Tagger. The bear took it in his jaws with gentle manners. His sizable teeth came close to Firth's hand, but Firth never flinched.

"Oh my," Eve whispered, as he slowly stroked the bear's wide forehead. Tagger lumbered away at a placid pace, carrying his prize. Doc Firth and he had an under-standing. Share the sweetness.

A sweet-talking man. So irresistible that even wild bears were charmed, and straw-berries ripened on his tongue.

Doug, Doctor to the Lost and Found

Alberta and Macy hand out "life mottos" on little business cards. I have a few stuck to the sun visor of my truck. I didn't put them there. Alberta and Macy did. With superglue.

Don't follow the path. Blaze a trail.
Live to be of value.

And my favorite:

Whatever you are, be a good one.

They called themselves "light workers" and "energy channels," which always makes me think of moths and light bulbs. I like all their talk of vortexes and spirits and dimensions because it makes everything seem so fixable and airy, but truth be told, my favorite cable show is *Mythbusters,* and I start every morning reading the Snopes website on my iPad to see what new gidgety blap has been revealed as a lie, a half-truth, or at least an unprovable notion.

But when I saw Tallulah Bankhead MacBride protecting her little girl at the risk of losing a kneecap or two, I decided Alberta and Macy were right about these ancient Appalachian Mountains. They block out the rest of the world and focus our attention right in front of us. Don't step off that ledge. Watch out for that snake. Be careful in those river rapids.

Don't take your eyes off the majesty of God's blue-green magic.

The steepest mountain sides are stuffed with thick evergreens and rise so high that sunlight barely reaches the forest floor and then, only at mid-day. If you want to blaze any trails, you better watch out for the noonday shadows.

The sunshine came down in a wide, soft beam on me and Tal as she introduced herself and Eve. She glowed. She took my breath away.

And though I tried to make a joke of it, I felt the heat.

I'm no' the pick of the litter, so they say. Lanky and bony and too fond of a dash of bitters in my beer, I am. What made a woman as fine as her give me an up-and-down that burned my skin?

Must've been the maternal urge. Saving her wee one from the cupcake-eatin' bear, I was.

Do you notice my Scots brogue gets stronger when I'm attracted to a special woman?

There hasn't been a special woman in my life for four years now. My wife divorced me during "the proceedings," as we called them down in Florida, and for a time, I thought I'd failed as a man. No matter the

44

selfish reason she walked out, unhappy that I'd thrown away my future among the high society of the horse-racing world, nor the praise I got for blowing the whistle on a company that had imported me from Scotland to keep its race horses "healthy," if by that you mean "making money." I had loved and lost the American woman to whom I'd pledged Forever. I was raised Presbyterian by Grandmama back in Glasgow, and we Scots Presbyterians take failure as a sign of personal weakness. I sank into drink and drugs for a mite after the divorce, the court battles, and the fight to keep my license. If not for Delta Whittlespoon and her biscuits, I might be buried inside a bottle now.

When she wrote to me, I thought, *What a strange woman!* Naturally, being a fey Scotsman, given to impulses, and hypnotized by the biscuits she sent me, I arrived in the Cove a week later.

My only regret? I didn't move here sooner.

Now, about Tal MacBride. A woman alone with a little girl, speaking with a hint of a local drawl but driving with New York State license plates. Heading for the Cove, she said, but she didn't share much else.

Another of Delta's stray puppies, I'm bettin'. Like me.

I'm good at taking care of stray pups.

Tal Meets the Yarn Fairy of Rainbow Goddess Farm

"Lucy," she introduced weakly, as she collapsed into the Bronco's passenger seat. "Lucy Parmenter."

"Tal and Eve," I replied. "MacBride."

"Nice to meet you," she groaned, then craned her head out of the ruined window and threw up.

Lucy Parmenter was delicate, blond, and damaged. I immediately liked her, worried about her, and wondered what terrible thing had turned her into a recluse who hyperventilated whenever she left Alberta and Macy's refuge, Rainbow Goddess Farm.

I would learn later that her background was different from the other women who came there for help. She hadn't been beaten and stalked by a boyfriend or husband; she had been brutally raped, beaten and robbed by two meth addicts who worked as maintenance men at her apartment complex. Her injuries were severe; she'd spent a month recovering at a hospital in her eastern Carolina hometown of Charlotte, where she'd taught art at a private school. Her late father had been a prominent Methodist minister. She had been sheltered, idealistic, and kind. The men who attacked her said they thought she "wanted it." Why? Because she'd taken time to talk to them as they made their regular rounds. She'd tried to counsel them. She'd brought them home-made soup on cold days and iced tea in the summer. She had extended the ministering welcome of food and faith, and, in return, they'd nearly killed her.

She was twenty-four when the attack took place. Now she was twenty-six. She sat among the dull pebbles of broken glass scattered around the Bronco's passenger seat as if she barely felt their rough texture through the strange outfit she wore: a heavy outdoor coat, a baggy denim jumper that went to her ankles, and sweat pants. Around her neck was the most beautiful wool scarf I'd ever seen. Silky, intricately woven in soft shades of gold and blue.

She downed a pill from the pocket of her heavy coat, pushing aside the gorgeous scarf to reach it. I drove slowly along the winding road that descended into the Cove, trying to give her time to recover from what she called "one of my tizzies." Also, I wanted information.

"Are you really a bunny?" Eve asked her from the back seat.

Lucy managed a frail laugh. "No, that's just my nickname. Everybody who lives where I live has a nickname. It's sort of a . . . club."

The nicknames were code to help hide the farm's guests from their stalkers. Macy was their licensed therapist. Alberta had been a paramedic in the marines. She was a skilled farmer, sustainable living guru, Jill of all trades, and devoted wife/husband to Macy, her partner of many years. Eventually, I would understand that Alberta was all about defending her weaker sisters — and brothers.

Lucy told us more.

The residents at Rainbow Goddess stayed there for little, if any, cost. They worked at the farm for their board. The main crop was berries of various kinds, but they also milked cows and goats, tended fields of corn, cabbage and other vegetables, and shared academic skills in small classes.

"We sell jams, jellies, cheese, butter, milk soap, and fiber." Lucy pointed to her scarf. She spoke in a soft, sophisticated southern accent, the kind I remembered being called "flatlander," by Asheville people. "I'm the resident spinner and knitter. Doctor Firth trades us a large share of the fleece at each shearing in return for us taking care of his sheep."

Doc Firth. A veterinarian.

"How long have you lived at the farm?"

"Two years." She hesitated, then . . . "Most of the women stay a few months. But I've become . . . somewhat permanent." A wistful tone of defeat seeped from those words.

Eve reached between our seats. In her small hand was the only surviving cupcake. "My mommy's the best baker ever! She sells cupcakes to movie stars and rich people in New York. Her cupcakes are magic! Would you like a Monkey Poop?"

Lucy brushed a wisp of blond hair from her eyes and studied the bright yellow icing, sniffing the air delicately. "That smells incredible!"

"Banana," I explained. "Give it a try. I'm pretty certain Tagger didn't drool on it."

Lucy took the proffered goodie in hands that looked chapped and callused. There was a gracefulness about her that made me cringe inside. How could anyone hurt her? "Oh, my," she said softly, raising the cupcake to her nose, inhaling. "I'll just take a nibble and give the rest back to you . . ."

Sixty seconds later, the only thing left was yellow cake crumbs scattered on her scarf. She looked from them to the empty paper cup. "I am *so* sorry! I just . . . zoned out and gobbled the whole thing! I'm so embarrassed!"

Eve and I chuckled. "Happens all the time," I said.

"What is this . . . a spell? You're a professional baker or a wizard? Wizardess?"

"I never graduated from cooking school, but yes. Cooking is a family tradition."

"Like Mommy's Cousin Delta," Eve said.

"You're related to Delta?"

"Distantly. She and my mother are eighth cousins twice remembered, or something like that. Connected through Mary Eve Nettie. My mother's middle name is 'Eve.'" I gestured toward the back seat. "That's why I gave the name to my little cupcake pusher."

"Cupcake pusher," Eve said merrily.

"You're here for a visit?"

"It's more like . . . we were visiting Asheville and decided to drop by." A small lie. "I've never met Delta." The truth.

"Oh. You didn't call ahead? She's not here right now."

I almost stomped the brake. We were coming off a sharp curve, not so much "descending" from Little Sheba, but sliding down her side. "She's not home?"

"No. And here's the irony. You drove down from New York. Well, that's where she is."

I groaned silently. "Why?"

"She's a contestant on *Skillet Stars*. The

50

show on the Kitchen TV Network? She's made it to the finals."

Oh, my god. I'd made it such a habit to avoid seeing, hearing, or reading about Mark that I was clueless about his latest enterprises. He owned a stake in several Kitchen TV shows including the hugely successful *Skillet Stars*. Every chef who'd won the grand prize — a one-season contract for his or her own show on the network — had gone on to fame and fortune.

Delta was in the finals? Mark and his evil sister, Twain, had tons of personal files on every contestant. And here I was, trying to hide out right under their noses. I might wreck Delta's chances. But how likely was it that they could figure out I was a cousin of hers?

Sweat beaded on my face. "I have to get my heater adjusted." I rolled down my window a few inches. With my luck, Tagger would fly through the air and attach himself to the moving SUV. Nothing was going as planned.

"Oh, Mommy, *look*," Eve sighed.

In my daze, I had not noticed. We cruised out of the lap of Little Sheba and into the Crossroads Cove.

It was as if a hidden kingdom wrapped us in its arms.

I'd seen photographs and paintings online — the Cove and the café were favorite subjects of local artists — but the quiet majesty of the place brought tears to my eyes. It was a small, flat valley surrounded by mountains. Pastures spread on each side. A creek bisected them, lined with bare trees and shrubs. Cattle, horses, sheep, and goats grazed on the brown November grass. An oasis of buildings were clustered at the base of the lower hills, swaddled in shade trees and nestled in the mountains' arms. Patches of evergreens brightened the gray forests. The slate-gray sky and rising mist gave everything a patina of vintage silver.

Maybe, despite the problems, we could be safe here.

When Eve reached between the seats to stroke Lucy's scarf, Lucy pulled it off and wrapped it around Eve's shoulders like a shawl. "Welcome to the Cove," she said.

CHAPTER TWO

Tal Learns About Christmas at the Café

Whittlespoons obviously *loved* Christmas. The Crossroads Café looked like a glowing spaceship with a veranda for a command deck. The place had more glitter, more shimmer, more all-out twinkle than a room full of female impersonators getting ready for a Las Vegas show.

The gracious old farmhouse was *covered* in Christmas decor. Fragrant woodsmoke curled from two stone chimneys. I wondered if there was any danger they'd set the holiday stuff on fire. A full-sized plastic sleigh, Santa, and eight reindeer perched on the main roof. Multi-colored Christmas lights flickered on all the eaves and window frames. Giant Christmas wreaths, plastic inflatable Santas, snow globes, snowmen, and elves bobbed in the breeze accompanied by the hiss of various air compressors. Giant plastic figures were *everywhere* — the veranda, the yards, the corners of the dirt parking lots, like a village of inflated cartoon characters about to come to life. There were even several in the pasture that bordered the trees as if they'd been fenced in to keep the cows company.

All the strings of lights were set on full twinkle even though it was daylight. Fake snow had been sprayed on every window and door pane. An entire row of large cedar trees on the parking lot's left edge were decorated in giant plastic ornaments, lights, and huge glitter stars.

Topping it all off: under one of the biggest oaks of the side yard sat a full-sized Nativity scene. It appeared to have been carved from logs via a chain saw.

The baby Jesus was covered in bark.

Eve squealed with joy. "It hurts my eyes!"

I had to admit, there was a major charm factor. Also a slight chance of retina damage.

"Joe Whittlespoon is in charge of all holiday décor," Lucy said as I pulled into a large, graveled lot. "He's Delta's brother-in-law. Her husband's older brother. He looks like a hippy version of Santa. He wears a *Grateful Dead* t-shirt under his Santa coat. Rumor has it that he . . . how can I put this in mixed company? *Indulges in some special cigarettes* while he decorates. Alberta says

54

Pike will find him just standing on his ladder beside the eaves, smiling at a string of lights in his hand."

I understood how the wattage could add to a psychedelic experience. And yet, a sense of welcome radiated from the glow. The café embraced me; so did the cluster of related buildings next door. No two were the same; some were little more than all-weather sheds, but all were folksy and friendly. GOOD FOOD AND MORE, said a weathered aluminum sign hanging from the café's eaves.

The "more" included a post office, Bubba's Pottery Studio And Gun Repair, a market stand with RAINBOW GODDESS FARMS on its sign, Smoochie's Swap And Thrift, Joe's Groceries And Wine Shop, The Café Gift Shop, and, in a weathered gray barn down the way a hundred yards, Whittlespoon Feed and Seed.

In front of Santa's/Joe's small grocery were two aging gas pumps, an ice machine, and what appeared to be a gigantic cage with a trip-wired door. A hand-printed sign was duct-taped to the steel-chain sides.

Rent this wild hog trap for $15 per week (or barter for the rent by promising Joe some sausage).

The specific offerings of this funny little shopping mall were listed on a tall sign at the edge of the road.

Welcome to the Crossroads Cove

Established in 1832 by Billings Jefferson and Tawah Turtle Jefferson at the crossing of the Asheville Trace and Ruby Creek Trail. Purchased fair and square from Tawah's tribe in exchange for discounts at the Crossroads Trading Post. Go twenty miles straight ahead to visit Turtleville, seat of Jefferson County. Go sixty-five miles backwards, to visit Asheville. Tennessee state line is "thataway."

What We Offer

**Home cooking and Delta's World-Famous Biscuits!
Groceries/Gas/Diesel/Kerosene/Propane
Beer and Wine (package sales only, for now)
Hardware/Farm Supplies
Camping/Fishing/Hunting Gear
Bait, Buck lure, and Bear Repellent
Post Office, Fireworks**

**Gem Shop, Pottery, Produce, Jellies,
Yarn and Other!
Cabin Rentals and Camp Sites
Maps/Books/Music
AND WIRELESS INTERNET**

I pulled into the parking lot and cut the Bronco's engine. Somewhere, emanating from a hidden speaker, came the most classic and sentimental of yuletide songs. *Grandma Got Run Over By A Reindeer.*

Tal to the Rescue

"Today's biscuits are in *Idaho.*"

That peculiar and frantic-sounding claim was yelled by a pear-shaped woman with wild brown hair and a cook's apron embroidered with THE LARD COOKS IN MYSTERIOUS WAYS AT THE CROSSROADS CAFÉ on the front. Her denimed legs pumped quickly as she bounded across the front parking area. I pushed Eve slightly behind me. The woman ran up to Lucy, gesturing wildly. "Dear Jesus, Bunny! They got routed the wrong way out of New York. No biscuit delivery today!"

Lucy backed up a couple of steps, going pale again. "It's a Monday. Aren't Monday nights in late fall pretty slow? I thought the dining room closed early on Mondays . . ."

"Not tonight! We've got a hundred people comin' from the Mountain View Resort over in Turtleville. Special reservation they made back in the summer! It's the fall conference of Western Carolina All-Church Music Ministers and Golf Club!" The woman raised her flour-dusted hands to the cloudy sky. "Jesus, I never asked to be in charge while Delta is up in New York City. Why has thou forsaken our biscuits?"

Lucy pivoted toward me. She wobbled a little. "Delta ships boxes of fresh-made biscuits to the café every day. It's the only way she'd agree to stay in New York for the past six weeks and compete on *Skillet Stars*. Cathy Mitternich — her manager — rented a commercial kitchen in Manhattan so Delta can do her baking. People come here for the famous Delta Whittlespoon biscuits. Substitutes won't do." She gulped for air. "But this is an emergency. You make amazing cupcakes. Can you, by any chance, make southern-style biscuits?"

"Whoa!" the other woman said hotly. " 'Scuse me, Bunny, but you're asking some *stranger* to take over the kitchen tonight?" To me she said, "No offense, but who in Jesus' Name *are* you?"

I hadn't come here to broadcast my name, my mission, or my family connection to

58

anyone but Delta. I should be meek, humble, dig the toe of my pink Croc in the soft dirt of this parking lot and say, *I'm just a visitor. I can't promise you much beyond an edible baked good.*

But I was tired of being dismissed as a flake. Yes, I would always be the flighty baby of the MacBride sibling trio, the one who loved neither wisely nor well, but here, now, in this emergency, a baker was needed.

I was all that and a bag of dough.

I raised my chin. "My name is Tallulah Bankhead MacBride, and I'm a trained baker. I am the daughter of Jane Nettie MacBride, and . . ."

The aproned woman looked at me suspiciously. "Jane Nettie of Asheville? She ran the B P and S Diner."

". . . who was taught to bake biscuits by Mary Eve Nettie, the same as she taught Delta . . ."

". . . you better be telling the truth."

"And so" — I raised a hand, palm out and up, in glorious testimony to the Holy Crusted Orb — "point me toward the kitchen and get me an apron."

A Passion, a Purpose, a Goat
Doug Observes . . .

Since there were five of us traipsing back and forth, not to mention two waitresses up front and a cashier, the café's kitchen was a warm beehive of Hurry where tasty aromas rose up out of big pots and skillets, pans clattered, and everyone tried to study Tal MacBride without Tal noticing. Including me.

Watching this mysterious visitor make biscuit dough hypnotized me in more ways than one. She massaged it oh-so-light and fine. She stroked it. She even whispered to it, bending over the long wooden dough board of the kitchen with tendrils of red hair curling from beneath a hairnet and purple knitted head band with colorful bobbles on it. Her passion held me like a magnet. Never had a woman cast a spell on me so quick and so innocently. I had to step out to the porch off the pantry from time to time to let the evening chill calm me down.

Distraction. I needed one.

"May I whisk this mischievous daughter of yours outside?" I asked her. "She's being far too well-mannered and quiet for my tastes."

Tal raised shining eyes to mine. It was as if she'd been lost in prayer, caught up in ecstasy. Her eyes had dilated with concentration, showing vivid green around the dark irises. Her face was flushed across the nose and cheeks. Her skin glistened with the damp heat rising off the pots of vegetables cooking on one of the stoves, and her lips were parted.

Dear God, to have her look at *me* like that instead of at biscuit dough.

She blinked and came back to earth. "Eve's spent a lot of time in commercial kitchens. She understands that it's not safe for her to move around."

Eve was a wee, sly sweetheart. She grinned up at me from a chair near the back door where she doodled with Crayons on a big notepad. "What's outside, Doctor Firth?"

Very polite.

I said politely back, "Call me Doug, Miss Eve. What's outside is a wily little goat named Teasel. He's kind of become my mascot. 'Twas born a bit early and too small. I fed him with a bottle and let him sleep on my bed amongst my dogs and cats. Now he thinks he's one of them. I half expect him to bark or meow."

Her face lit up. "Mommy, can I go?"

A hint of concern clouded her eyes. Me, a stranger of the male variety, disappearing outdoors with her daughter. I said quickly,

"Just right outside the door here on the side porch. No farther. The light's on. Come stand at the window and watch as I make the introductions. Or step outside. 'Tis brisk, not too cold."

"All right, then. Eve, wrap up good in your new scarf."

She hopped off the chair excitedly and wrestled with the scarf, which was very long for a child to wear.

"Here, may I help?" I asked. Tal secured me with a nod of permission. I bent to Eve. "Hold this end in your hands, and I'll hold the other. Then you spin about — don't get addled and fall down! — and I'll wind the scarf around you like a yarn burrito!"

She giggled. A minute later she twirled to a stop, wobbling and laughing and bundled not so much like a burrito with blue jeaned legs, but rather a blue and gold puffball. She peered at me with only her eyes and nose showing and waved her hands, which stuck out beneath the bottom side of the scarf. I tucked a top corner down the back of her neck. "There. And the extra thing is you're well-padded in case Teasel butts you. I believe you'll just bounce."

With her chortles muffled behind yarn, I guided her to the porch. Tal stepped out behind us. I felt her gaze on me, and my skin tingled with more than the brisk air. A soft gold sunset lingered over Ten Sisters, and the late autumn nightfall had turned the side yard's big shade trees into patterns of lacy branches against a blue-black sky, backlit by the last of the light.

Across the way, Joe Whittlespoon's carved-log Nativity characters stared at their woody Christ child. Rotating spotlights of red and green moved across the carved hickory faces of the wise men, the pine-scented Mary and Joseph, the camel made of oak logs, and several log-and-tree-branch deer, which were not historically accurate. I pointed at them. "Santa Joe thinks Bethlehem had a deer-hunting season."

A soft sound came from the shadows. I turned to find Tal laughing. What a warm and lovely bit of music.

Clackety clackety clank clank clank thud. "Bahhhh."

Eve screeched lightly. She dodged a small black goat with a white blaze between his china-blue eyes. Teasel liked to bounce. To hop. And so he sailed out of the shadows of the yard onto the small porch, scattering several empty gallon cans waiting to go in the trash. He halted to gaze up at Eve. He liked children, especially the ones who were easy to knock down. He waggled his head

63

at her. A warning sign. "Bah." It sounded like a challenge.

"No, no, Teasel, bad Teasel," I commanded, stepping over to block him.

"BAAAAAHHH," Eve shouted back at him. She lowered her head and butted him on one shoulder.

Teasel bounded off the porch, flipped around, went "Baaaahhh," and bounced back up.

"Bahhhh!" She butted him again.

He butted her in the stomach.

"Bah!" she squealed, and launched herself at him again.

The next thing we knew, Eve and Teasel were off the porch and on the ground together, chasing each other around the side yard under the light of the security lamp. They traded more butts and bahs. He hopped. She hopped.

I pivoted to look at Tal, worrying that she might want to headbutt *me* for introducing her child to Hippity Hop The Attack Goat. She clamped a flour-dusted hand to her mouth, and her eyes were wide.

Then she burst out laughing. She laughed in long gulps, bending over, holding her stomach. I laughed too, just out and out roaring with it, something I hadn't done in years. I guffawed. I slapped my chest. Staggering, we somehow managed to collide at the shoulders, which only made us laugh harder. Eve and Teasel were still butting each other in the yard, and their new game had spread to us like an airborne elixir.

Finally we could only manage the strangled *he-he-he* people emit right before they began gasping and coughing. Red-faced and grinning like mad, we did what old friends do when their bones have gone soft from lack of oxygen. We propped ourselves on each other. I draped an arm around her shoulders. She didn't pull away. She leaned into me and even patted me on the front of my plaid shirt.

I pointed at Eve and Teasel. "I hate to inform you, Mrs. MacBride, but your child is clearly a full kissing cousin to yon goat. Does her father have cloven hooves?"

Her laughter drained off. Her eyes snapped. She eased from under my friendly arm. My excellent sensitivity to a woman's changing moods rang a loud alarm. I had my own brand of foul language for hard times, and I liked to think it was more charming than crude. It came in handy as her body language rolled through my brain.

I'm fecked. Completely fecked. She's fecking mad at me. Feck.

"I'm not married," she informed me.

"And Eve's father probably does have cloven hooves. Also a forked tail and red horns."

"I'm sorry for upsetting you."

She shook her head. "Not your fault. Thanks for the laugh." She nodded toward Eve and Teasel, who were still butting and bouncing. "I have to go back to my biscuits. You'll stay out here and make sure she doesn't hurt him? I think her head's harder than his."

"I'll be right here. Don't you worry. You can trust me, Tal. If you feel like telling me what's up with this visit of yours . . ."

Her eyes went darker, the way they had when she looked at the dough. I stopped talking. She was studying me, what I was made of. Suddenly the moment was close, intimate, filled with the kind of personal scrutiny that can segue, very quickly, into a kiss. My god, I'd only known her a few hours. I wasn't lubed with alcohol or drugs, and I was beginning to shiver because I'd left my coat inside. And yet I felt hot and giddy.

Her breath came quick. A bit agitated, in a good way, I hoped. "This is going to sound strange," she said, beginning to frown. "But . . . some people have an odd talent. They see colors around people.

66

Auras. They see colors that go with sounds and emotions. All sorts of things. I have . . . a similar . . . oddness. Sometimes, people give off a scent. Not a real scent you can smell in the air. More of . . . an emotional scent. It's in my mind."

She was clearly embarrassed about the admission. I would never make fun of woo-woo notions. I have a few myself, and besides, in the Cove, "woo woo" is a daily occurrence. Just like in Asheville, where they sell t-shirts that say, "It's not weird, it's Asheville."

"Do I have a good scent?" I asked.

"Scotch whiskey and cinnamon buns."

A compliment. Definitely. A good thing. A grand thing, even.

She wasn't married. She wasn't in love with Eve's father, and I brought hungry thoughts to her.

The kitchen door burst open. Cleo stuck her head out and scowled at us. Cleo is the one who'd run outdoors earlier, yelling about the biscuits heading to Idaho. She was Delta's sister-in-law. Married to Delta's husband's brother, Charlie "Bubba" Whittlespoon. Cleo's a good person, no nonsense, cares a lot about the family, the biscuits, the reputation. She'll guard your back in a fight. But she's not necessarily the

67

most relaxed person to leave in charge. Not even with Jesus as her assistant.

Cleo snorted. "Delta never leaves *her* biscuits alone in the oven."

"I'm coming in right now." Tal went back inside.

Leaving me hungry, too.

Doug's Fingers Are Crossed . . . for the Biscuit Test

Everyone was on pins and needles about the outcome of Tal's biscuits. There was no backup plan if her first batch looked like leftovers from one of those cardboard tubes of processed dough you buy at the super-market. Too late to close down for the night.

Cars started rolling into the front lot; the dining rooms began to fill with noisy, happy people. Pots of coffee and pitchers of sweet iced tea were carried out to greet them. No beer or wine, though Delta had been pondering the addition, just as soon as Jefferson County approved it by the drink. I myself would like to see a good rowdy pub in the vicinity. I was still known to down a beer or three.

"We'll need the first batch of biscuits in no more than five minutes. *Five* minutes!" Cleo said to Tal, coming over from the casserole oven to hover and pace near the biscuit oven.

"Ready," Tal said calmly. She swirled a dish towel around her hand, swooped down like a curvy ballerina and opened the oven door.

Curtain up. Lots of breaths were held. The fry cook, Arnold, the grill cook, Bubba, and the salad chopper, Jenny, looked like stop-action figures with the batteries turned off. All eyes went to that open oven door.

"Come to me, you big, handsome boys," Tal said. She pulled out a large baking tray. On it stood row after row of fat, fluffy, golden-brown biscuits. In the Biscuit Olympics, she'd just won the Gold at least for presentation.

"They look passable," Cleo said haughtily. As if everyone weren't awed. "But now for the taste test." She snatched two biscuits up, yipping as the buttery heat hit her fingertips. "Here." Half to Bubba. Half to Arnold. The other biscuit was split between Jenny and Cleo. I glanced beside me at Eve, who was wiggling on her chair and grinning at her mother proudly.

Tal had already gone back to seducing another mound of dough. Confidence. *Talk dirty to that bad boy, lass. Slap it and rub some butter on the bulges and . . .*

"Jesus H. Christ!" Arnold said, chewing

the biscuit with a look of ecstasy on his face. A biscuit so good it made a church goer backslide. He had spiked hair, a nose ring, and a neck tattoo that said *Saved* under a crucifix.

"Arnold!" Cleo hissed.

"I'm sorry Miz McKellan, but this is as good as Delta's!"

"Do not take that name in vain!"

Not sure whether she meant Jesus or Delta. Or both.

Silence. Stark, prickly, and shocked. I did a quick survey of Bubba's face. His eyebrows shot up, and he turned back to his grill, wiping biscuit crumbs off the hairnet covering his gray-brown beard. A wise man. Avoiding confrontation.

Jenny, the salad chopper, hid her last bite of biscuit in a pocket of her apron and said, "I best go wash this butter off my fingers." She fled to the outside bathroom, which was mostly used by staff and family. We called it The Privy of Fine Art, and it was famous.

Cleo stared at the biscuit she hadn't sampled yet. As if tasting toxic waste, she sniffed it, stuck a tiny bit in her mouth, bit that off with her teeth, and pretty much swallowed the sample without chewing. She dropped the rest in a trash can. "They'll do," she said, "but they're not up to Delta's standards." She stomped out.

Tal hummed and went back to kneading dough.

Tal's Memories of Mama and Apple Pie

I wasn't worried about my biscuits. Baking came to me naturally. I simply channeled Mama and Mary Eve Nettie. Mama's aunt was an early feminist, environmental activist, life-long goat-and-sheep shepherdess, seducer of younger men, and a pure-T wizardly alchemist in the kitchen.

Aunt Mary Eve died of a stroke in nineteen seventy-nine (she was seventy-two by then) while leading an anti-Reagan rally in downtown Asheville. Some say she pushed herself too hard, that she shouldn't have been smoking so much weed or gotten that last tattoo on her aging shoulders, the big one of the haloed biscuit shooting rays lined with the Cherokee syllabary. Can a person seriously translate "Fear No Weevils" into Cherokee?

At any rate, she left her magic in good hands: Mama's and Delta's. There aren't Six Degrees of Separation between Southern cousins. There is only one degree: family.

"Baaah," Eve said softly, back in her chair by the café's kitchen door.

I turned to see if Teasel had sneaked inside. Instead I found her and Doug wiggling their fingers atop their heads and butting the air at each other. He glanced at me and smiled. Scotch and cinnamon, yes. His aroma curled deep inside me. "Cleo's coming back," he explained. "You best look biscuit-ish."

"Baah," Eve repeated, and butted the air. He did the same again. This big, brawny Scotsman did not seem to fear looking delightfully silly. He'd named their game "Bad Goat." When Arnold the Fry Cook made the mistake of praising my biscuits, I glimpsed Eve and Doug signaling *Bad Goat* at each other.

He'd known my daughter for only a few hours, yet they were comfortable together.

Forget About Cleo, Real Trouble Has Arrived

Midnight. Eve was curled up asleep under the chair with Doug's fleece-lined coat wrapped around her. My hands ached from kneading so much dough. My shoulders throbbed. My arms felt like rubber. If there is a Guinness world record for Most Biscuits Made From Scratch In One Evening, I'd win it.

Over five hundred biscuits. Except for the

plate of ten that Bubba had hidden for himself when Cleo wasn't looking, all had been eaten on site, purchased for take-out by one hundred very happy golfers from the resort in Turtleville, or saved to serve to the breakfast and lunch crowds tomorrow.

"We made more money in tips tonight than in a whole entire weekend during the best part of fall leaf season!" proclaimed Danielle, the fraternal twin sister of the other waitress, Brittany. Both were dressed as elves.

Everyone was happy except Cleo, who stared at me as if I'd spray-painted gang symbols on the side of a church. "Here. Twelve dollars an hour for seven hours' work. Thanks for helping out. We'll be back on our biscuit delivery schedule tomorrow. Won't need you again." She handed me a wad of cash. Since I was helping Jenny, the salad chopper, wash pots and pans, I took a moment to dry my hands while I gazed stonily at the money.

"Divide it among the kitchen staff. I didn't do this for pay. I came here to visit Delta. I'm a cousin. This is a family operation."

Jenny looked up at me from over a steaming sink. Her brows flattened. She went from me to Cleo to me again. "Just for the

73

record," she drawled, "Tal, your biscuits are as good as Delta's. You've got the touch."

Cleo angrily stuffed the cash in a clean coffee mug. The impact rattled a metal prep table. "You show up here unannounced," she spat at me, "not calling ahead. You don't even know that Delta is up in New York — but that's where you're from — and yes, I grant you that your mama's reputation is a calling card, Bless Her Heart and May She Rest Easy In The Bosom Of The Lamb, but other than that, we don't know you from Adam's housecat, and Alberta Spruill-Groover says — and she has plenty of experience from studying women who are in trouble — Alberta says you're on the run from something. So why don't you quit pretendin' this is some sweet little visit to a cousin you never cared enough about to visit before, and 'fess up what you *really* want?"

"She wants to be treated with a bit o' respect and a nice big 'Thank you,' for saving your bacon tonight," Doug interjected. He'd stepped inside during Cleo's tirade. Cold air wafted off his flannel shirt. He'd helped out by bussing tables and toting garbage outside. His deep voice singed the air. He could look ferociously angry.

I wanted to adore him. Reckless, unqualified adoration, based on nothing but a few hours' superficial acquaintance. Hadn't I learned anything from trusting my impulses with Mark?

"Thank *you*," I said to Doug, and put a dishwater-pruned hand to my heart. I turned back to Cleo. "I'm glad to have helped out here in an emergency. Now Eve and I will be moving on. I'm sorry we missed seeing Delta." I folded the dish towel, took off my apron, and knelt by Eve on the floor. I stroked her red hair back from her face. She looked like a Celtic Eskimo, swaddled in a halo made by the thick fleece of the coat's collar. "Wake up, sweetie. Time to go."

She 'ummmed' and huddled deeper into Doug's coat.

"You're not thinkin' to get back on the road tonight, are you?" Doug asked grimly.

"Yes. I understand Turtleville isn't too far, and there are a couple of inns there . . ."

"It's on t'other side of the next mountain, and there's no need for you to make that drive. There's nice little cabins scattered about the cove, all for rental, and . . ."

"They're all occupied," Jenny put in sadly. "Since Jeb and Becka are up in New York City, I've been put in charge of 'em. Booked up. Sorry."

"Then Tal and Eve can stay at Delta's house. She's got plenty o' guest rooms, and I know she'd want them to stay."

"The house is locked up," Cleo snapped. "I'm in charge of it. I can't and won't give permission for strangers to use it. I say 'No.' "

"What's got into you, Cleo? Delta and her biscuits don't need you to fight for them. She'd be the first to say 'Good on you!' to Tal, here. And she'd welcome her to be a guest in her house."

I stood. Looking up at Doug's unforgettable face. I knew I needed to get far, far away from him before I lost all restraint and common sense and threw myself on him like butter on a hot muffin. "It's not good for us to be here. Not good for any of you, or this café, or for Delta. She has a lot at stake and I'm . . ." Too much information. "Look, I'm used to taking care of myself and my daughter without any backup plan." I hoped the words sounded gentle, not arrogant. No brag, just fact. "It's best that we leave."

He shook his head. "Let's step outside and have Teasel decide, how about that? I'll set out two flower pots. If he butts the one on the left, you stay. On the right, you go."

"I have a feeling you've taught him secret goat signals."

"Ah, you know me too well! I'm a goat-whisperer."

No, the problem is that I didn't know him well at all. My instincts might be perfect with baked goods, but they were disastrous with men.

Bubba stuck his head through the doorway to the dining room. His beard waggled in its net. "There's two men out here lookin' for Tallulah B. MacBride. I'd say they're trying real hard to seem way too casual about it. You expectin' any company?"

I froze. Everyone's eyes turned to me. Had Mark sent people to track me? How?

No choice. I glanced at Eve to confirm she was still sound asleep then looked at Doug. "I'm not a criminal. Please don't ask me to explain, at least not right now." I tilted my head, indicating Eve.

For a heartstopping moment he judged me shrewdly, and his jaw hardened. *Is he for me or against me?*

Cleo spouted, "I'm in charge here, and if those men are officers of the law, I'm going out there right now and be honest with them. I'm sorry, Tal, I truly am. But Delta's husband Pike is the sheriff of this county. I am duty-bound to cooperate with the Law. Right, Bubba?"

Her husband shuffled unhappily then

77

found his courage. "Hon, you want me to list all our kin who've got reason to avoid the Law? Starting with Joe and his weed patch?"

"Bubba! She's not kin, not really. Some high-falutin' distant cousin is all she . . ."

"I'll take responsibility for talking to the strangers," Doug said. "Put it on my shoulders. I'll do it."

"You sure, Doc?" Bubba looked relieved.

He gave me another indecipherable look, frowning, then shifted his gaze to Eve. "Are you on the up and up? Is this about protecting Eve? Just nod or shake."

I nodded.

"Then I'm your man."

Bubba stepped aside to let him ride out on his white horse.

Doug Gives Them More Than They Bargained For

I've some experience with trouble, and I've learned a thing or two from a lifetime of tending animals. Not so different from reading the moods of people. A shifty eye, a direct stare, a slight curl of the lip, or a certain tilt o' the head. Warning. Danger. Plus I know a bit about how mams treat their babes and how babes act around mams who are loving and patient.

Not to compare Tal MacBride to a cow, a mare, or a ewe, but as we say in the birthing sheds, *she gives milk with a lot o' heart in it.*

Whatever her problems, and whatever her blame for those problems, Tal MacBride was all about keeping her daughter safe. I was right there with her on that score. If she wanted to stay clear of the boys standing in the café's empty dining room, looking like attack dogs pretending to be lap dogs, she had some good reason.

"Hail and well met," I said to them. Nothing throws an attack dog off faster than an unexpected Scottish greeting. "I'm the manager. Doug Firth's the name." I held out a hand. "And you two gents would be . . . ?"

They smirked at me, smiling like I might bring out a banjo and start singing a Scots' version of *Coming Round the Mountain* or *My Hillbilly Ways Put The Love In Her Eyes* (a favorite vintage tune of mine, by the way). They shook my hand and introduced themselves. I filed away their names and noted their body language. *Fidgety,* I named one. *Shark Eyes,* I named the other.

Both were outfitted like the kind of hikers who only hike to a pool hall or strip joint. Trouble, yes.

"We're private investigators," Fidgety said, wiggling his fingers by his side. "We've been following a woman named Tallulah MacBride. We found her car in the parking lot here, tonight. New York State license tag. Ford Bronco. We'd just like to talk to her."

I decided to play stupid. Comes easy to me. "Well, now, you can see that we're closed for the night, and there's not a customer left in sight. We had a full house. Maybe she's rented a cabin around here. Or she's a golfer from Turtleville. This place was full to the rafters with 'em. Smelled like mowed grass and wet balls."

"Her car's still outside," Fidgety said, cracking his knuckles.

"Really? We've got an outside toilet — but with modern plumbing, I mean. It's a lean-to on the back of the house. Sometimes people hide in there to skip out on their bill. Or to have a bit o' fun. But we've got an attack goat on the premises, so I usually hear the screaming. Can you describe this Tallulah woman to me?"

"She's nearly six feet tall," said Shark Eyes. "With long red hair. A little on the chunky side. Big green eyes. A hint of a southern accent. Has a little bit of an overbite. She's hard to miss."

"Sounds like my kind o' woman. Is she alone?"

"She's got her daughter with her," Fidgety said, bumping the heel of one hand on his creased cargo pants. Who puts a crease in their cargo pants? "Long red hair, five years old, gawky, an overbite like her mother. Not a contestant for any little-girl beauty pageants."

"Not ringing a bell," I told them. "Maybe this 'Tallulah' found herself a friend among the golfers and caught a ride to a hot night on the town."

"Would you mind if we look around? Check that . . . what did you call it?"

"Privy. It's full name is The Privy of Fine Art. Sure." I jerked a thumb toward the front doors. "Out to the left, past the side porch, past the loading dock and the kitchen doors, and look out for the goat."

"The goat worries me," Fidgety said with a new smirk and a twitch in his right thumb. "How about we go through the restaurant and out the kitchen doors?"

Push had come to shove, or, as Grandmama Ardwyn O'Conner Firth used to say in Glasgow, *It's time to pull the wool out from under these feckers.*

"No, we'll protect you from the goat. No worries, gents."

Shark Eyes gestured toward the hall to the back. "Mind if I take a piss in the *indoor* toilet, first?"

"We're closed for the evening. Sorry."

"What happened to Southern hospitality?"

"I'm Scottish. So feck off."

Fidgety's face went dark. He took a step forward, flexing his shoulders. He was as tall as me with more muscle, and he did a good job of turning his nervous tics into menace. "Tallulah MacBride and her kid are here. We know it, and you know it, too. If you don't want the police involved, you'll hand her over."

Shark Eyes moved in on me, too. "There's a warrant for her arrest on assault charges. If the cops come, she's going to jail. But if she cooperates with us, we'll just escort her back to New York and let the lawyers handle it."

"Ah. Violent, is she? If I was you, I'd call the sheriff to come tase her and her child to boot. But Sheriff Whittlespoon is up in New York with the owner of this fine establishment. His *wife*. Besides, I'm pretty sure he'd tell you to get the feck out, too."

Fidgety took a swing at me. I was a boxer at university; nearly made the Scottish Olympic team. So I dodged pretty well and tapped him on the jaw. He fell backward and nearly knocked Shark Eyes down.

Shark Eyes pulled out a pistol.

I lunged for it. The loudest *blam* in five counties clubbed my eardrums. A ceiling fan exploded over Fidgety and Shark Eyes. Bits of brass and shredded wood rained down on them. Shark Eyes and Fidgety covered their heads and began backing toward the doors.

My ears ringing like mad, I turned around to see who'd gone all Annie Oakley on the three of us.

Cleo stood in the hallway to the kitchen, her favorite double-barreled shotgun to her shoulder. She sighted down the barrel with a Clint Eastwood squint. She was ready to aim lower the next time.

"Jesus loves you," she said to Fidgety and Shark Eyes. "But I'll shoot your peckers off."

Tal and Eve, Hiding in the Privy of Fine Art

"What was *that*?" Eve asked sleepily, sitting on the closed lid of a commode with strange blue trout painted all over it. Teasel stood beside her, eating a roll of toilet paper.

A gun shot. I slid a hand into the pocket of my pink hoodie with the cupcake embroidered on the back. My fingers closed around the Glock. "Oh, it's probably just a tree falling over. One of those big trees that shade the parking lot. Trees make a lot of noise when they go *boom*."

She yawned and rubbed her eyes. I stared at my stark-white face in the mirror of an old medicine chest surrounded by a mural of shiny rocks in the pattern of an arch. A Noah's Ark of folk-art animals roamed the toilet's beadboard ceiling and old plank walls.

"Gobble, gobble!" Eve laughed, reaching out to stroke one of the purple turkeys that lived in the walls of the commode nook.

I'd spent our time in the Privy braiding my hair in a fuzzy plait so she'd think I was calm. My ears strained. All that stood between us and capture was a creaky wooden door on which a herd of bright orange and green deer galloped into a giant setting sun rimmed in vintage beer-bottle tops.

Ninety degrees from the sun's apex (at Pabst Blue Ribbon) and five inches to the right of Schlitz, a frail metal hook latched the door to an eye bolt that wobbled when I poked it.

"Go hide in *The Privy of Fine Art*," Bubba had directed. "Last place anyone would look."

Unless the goons Mark sent were art critics.

Feet crunched on the gravel path outside. Multiple sets of feet. Feet moving fast. I faced the door, slipping the gun out. It was small enough to palm in my hand, hiding it from Eve. "Stay right here on the bathroom seat behind Mommy, okay?"

She stared at the door. "Somebody must need to go potty really bad!"

Tap tap tap. The door shivered, and so did I. "Come out, lady-girls," Doug called. "Staying in there too long will give a person bad gas and strange dreams."

My breath gushed in relief. I flipped the hook and flung the door open. Doug, Cleo, Bubba, Arnold, Jenny, Danielle and Brittany gazed back at me. Their arsenal included shotguns, rifles, handguns, and a hatchet. Doug was the only one not armed. Or maybe he was, only in a different way. I noticed the paper towel wrapped around his right hand. Blood stained it. My heart swelled. *He fought for us?*

His attention went to the Glock. Everyone else craned their heads to look, too. Cleo went "Hummph," in surprise.

"Was there some kind of . . . issue?" I asked Doug. *Please don't say anything scary in front of Eve.*

"Not a bit. Tagger came wandering about, looking for more Monkey Poop, and Cleo scared him off with her shotgun."

"She shooted Tagger?" Eve wailed.

He leaned aside to smile down at her. "No worries, sweetheart. Not a hair was harmed on Tagger's furry black head."

"I promise, Hon," Cleo said. The shotgun propped on her shoulder bore a small brass plaque on its gleaming wooden stock. *Pray For Peace,* it said.

Pray I don't end up in pieces, I thought. *If she's still determined to get rid of me.*

"This settles it," Bubba announced, grinning at me. "Tal's hidin' in the Privy and packin' heat. She's a Whittlespoon cousin, for sure."

CHAPTER THREE

Tal and Eve's Excellent Adventure Begins in Free Wheeler

Fidgety and Shark Eyes were now tracking Eve and me to the Knoxville, Tennessee headquarters of the Cluck Burgers fast food chain. Fifty-five stores are scattered throughout the southeast, mostly in markets where they don't have to compete with the king of chicken burgers, Chick-fil-A.

Doug and Bubba discovered a tracking device stuck to the bottom of my Bronco. Bubba handed it to Arnold. Arnold's mother, Tiffany Darleen "Booty" Davis, drives a tractor-trailer for Cluck Burgers. He rushed home and gave the device to her before she left on her two a.m. schedule.

"Oh, hell yeah, I'll take care of this New World Order gadget," Booty said. She's a survivalist, a lifetime NRA member, president of the Jefferson County Tea Party, and a forum moderator at the *Tin Foil Hatters* blog, where the motto is: *We're not paranoid. We're para-prepared.* Once in Knoxville, she'd hand the tracker to a fellow driver. By tomorrow afternoon, Eve and I would be delivering frozen cluck patties to Louisville, Kentucky.

In the meantime, I accepted Doug's invitation to stay at his house for the night. Just one night, then I'd come up with Step Two of my haphazard non-plan. He described a comfortable guest bedroom — Eve and I would share it. No strings attached. I relaxed just enough to believe him. He continued to fill my mental aromatherapy channel with Scotch and cinnamon. Mark had inspired no scent at all. That should have warned me.

Besides, if Doug proved unworthy of my fledgling trust, I had my pistol.

Now we were in the middle of nowhere, heading toward his home in a deserted "bicycle village" that had once been known as Free Wheeler. No one would find us there, he promised. For sure. Not without a trail of bread crumbs and a satellite. How much time did I have before Mark's repo men caught up with us again?

"This is where the original road starts," Doug said loudly. Tree branches tickled the windshield. We had forded two shallow creeks, gone up and down hills, and now what had been little better than a hunting trail suddenly turned into a bumpy obstacle course. "O'r the years since Free Wheeler became a ghost town, the pavement's crumbled quite a bit," Doug went on. "In places it's gotten right down to the cobblestone layer underneath. That part dates to about nineteen twenty, when young Arlo Claptraddle started building his fey dream of a bicycle wonderland."

"Arlo Claptraddle? That can't be his real name."

"Likely not. He loved theatrics. Quite a showman, they say. Some called him 'the Walt Disney of bicycles.' Whoever he really was, he had a passion for his work, and he followed his heart. That's what drew me to the place. I like to be certain of what I want and who I am." He cut his eyes at me when he said that.

The truck lurched over a hummock of cracked pavement. Eve squealed and laughed. We all bounced. "So you took the road less paved?"

Doug grinned and went on, "They say he built the first section of this lane with his own two hands. Up yon you'll be seeing a replica of the Welcome sign he put in. Pike Whittlespoon has some old photos that Grandpa Whittlespoon took. I created a new sign by copying the one in his pictures."

He was practically shouting as the rumbling and bouncing grew worse.

Eve went, "Ah ah ah ah ah, oh oh oh oh, buh buh buh buh . . ."

Curled up beside her on the seat, Teasel went, "Bahba bahba bahba bah."

I clutched my seatbelt. "Are we in Oz yet? Are we still in North Carolina? Are we traveling back in time?"

Doug laughed — a deep, rich, wonderful sound. "Free Wheeler's just 'round the side of this mountain. We're nearly home." He said *home* as if it was our home, too. "There's the Welcome sign, see?" He pointed as the headlights illuminated a small clearing in the forest.

Two handsome stone pillars rose on either side of the narrow concrete and stone lane. Atop them, bridging the way, a banner-shaped metal sign blazed with cheerful paint colors and vintage lettering. The effect reminded me of classic circus posters and carnival advertisements. Below a detailed painting of a Victorian couple riding a two-seater bicycle, the text read:

Greetings! Welcome to the glorious village of Free Wheeler, North Carolina!

Home of the Clapper Bicycle Emporium!

Magical motion machines are brought to life here!

Take your dreams for a spin!

Arlo Claptraddle, proprietor, fantasist, inventor, ad hoc mayor

A welcome committee of animals appeared along the fences and in the lane. A dozen dogs, a few cats, two small pigs, several llamas, ducks, chicken, a pair of geese, and a great horned owl who landed atop a fence post, looking wise.

"Doctor Doolittle lives here!" Eve said. "Look, Mommy! A big doll house!"

An alley of replica Victorian streetlamps led us forward; the clearing expanded into a small pasture rimmed in white fences. A floodlight illuminated a large barn with stone sides and a shingled roof. A grove of enormous oak trees made a wide semi-circle at the edge of deep forest. The gentle folds of the mountains' skirts created knolls and hollows. A pretty creek trickled beneath us as we drove over a wooden bridge.

Nestled in a shady hollow was, indeed, a life-size dollhouse, complete with a turret, gingerbread trim, stained glass transoms over the windows, and a long veranda.

"She's a pretty old lady, is she not?" Doug said. "I've spent three years restoring the darlin', per Tom Mitternich's architectural notes and Jay Wakefield's budget. 'Twas Arlo's house. Another few minutes up the lane and you'll see the old bicycle factory and shops he built for his community of employees. I'll show you in the daylight, if you've a mind to take a look."

"Yes!" I said eagerly, and he smiled.

Bonding with Doug, in the Barn

It was three a.m. Eve slept soundly in a plain but comfortable guest room. Teasel curled up atop the blanket at her feet, as if he were a dog. He dozed and snored.

"Is that you?" Doug asked from the shadows of his barn. He was feeding Zanadu, a race horse he'd rescued, and Pammy, a Shetland pony missing one ear.

I stepped into the light of the barn's central hall, carrying a bucket. "Yep."

"You're a farm girl?"

"Sort of. I was raised by people who had a small ranch."

"And where would that have been?"

I chewed my tongue. Careful. "I appreciate your help, I really do. But tomorrow, Eve and I will be leaving. It really is best I don't say more than that."

He hung up the feed bucket. "Suit yourself."

"I've fed all the other animals. Found the goat food, goose food, dog food, and the cat food. Wasn't sure what to feed the owl. He doesn't seem to be hungry, anyway. Doesn't give a hoot."

Doug smiled. "He was brought to me as a chick with a broken wing. I rehabbed him and turned him loose. He just comes back to visit." He shook the last grains from a bucket of feed into the trough shared by Zanadu and Pammy. "Thank you."

"It's the least I can do. Reimbursement for your hospitality."

"Here's the thing, though." He ruffled Zanadu and Pammy's forelocks as they dug their noses into the grain. "The spirit of the Cove, which includes this forgotten community here, is about togetherness and graciousness and acceptance. It's no' about paybacks." He paused, frowning gently. "It's about sharing the good and the bad. It's about kindness."

My throat locked with emotion. "I've got cookies baking in your oven," I said, and disappeared into the night.

Tal Gets a Call from Gabby in California

Four a.m. A pan of from-scratch oatmeal cookies sat on the stove top in his cozy kitchen. Me? Nibbling my fingernails. Wide awake. Wired.

Doug munched cookies and prepared something he called "gourmet late-night snacks." I sat at the aged wooden table in the kitchen's breakfast nook, beneath the soft light of a hanging lamp he'd made from a rusty bicycle wheel. Like the rest of the house, the kitchen was a mix of rundown areas and handsomely restored ones, of vintage charm and modern gizmos. He had a Keurig and a juicer but also an aluminum bread box and an old potbellied heater outfitted with gas jets. Around a dual-tub sink with brass fixtures were tall wooden cabinets. He'd restored the kitchen's counters to the sheen of the original wood. I dug my bare toes into a thickly braided rug on the wood floor. I loved the kitchen. I loved the house, messy and half-fixed, smelling of animals and bachelorhood. Houses have psychic aromas just like people. This one made me think of apple cider and roasting coffee beans.

"May I borrow a phone?" I asked Doug. "Mine is in my Bronco." The Bronco was hidden inside the loading area of Whittlespoon Feed and Seed.

"Surely." As he moved about his kitchen, he handed me the cell phone from a back pocket of his khakis. The phone's heavy-duty rubber case was missing one corner and had a toothy set of scrape marks on the back. "It's a tough trooper, that one. Saved me from an angry mare with sharp chompers."

I tried not to dart a look at his handsome rump. A Scottish brogue is charming enough by itself. He combined it with rugged good looks, a deep baritone, and a colorful way with words. It should be classified as a controlled substance. I began typing a text to Gabby. I felt him watching me. I owed him less secrecy and more explanations.

SAFE FOR 2 NITE. AT DELTA'S. BORROWED A PHONE. LUV TO U. U OK?

It was one a.m. in L.A. Gabby would be at work — a side job as a caterer, scraping together money to pay her legal bills. I didn't expect her to answer. She'd be in the middle of dishing out late-night hors d'ouevres and her special relishes.

LAY LOW!!!

Came the immediate reply.

E7 IS SNOOPING. I AM DODGING THEM. THEY WANT TO KNOW IF U R MARK'S BABY MAMA.

Clammy chills skittered across my forehead. My stomach rolled. I typed shakily,

UNDERSTOOD. CALL U 2MORROW. LUV. BYE

She came right back with:

TXT GUS SOON. HE HASN'T HEARD FROM U. HE IS GETTING WORRIED. CAN'T KEEP THIS SECRET MUCH LONGER. LV U, G'NITE

My fingers shaking more, I typed:

WILL DO. LV U 2.

She and I texted Gus almost every day.

We also sent him weekly care packages. We never skipped a mailing. I'd have to come up with something tomorrow.

I stared into space while taking a deep breath to settle my stomach. "E7" was short for "Entertainment 7," one of the most aggressive celebrity gossip sites. Tiny stars shot across my vision.

"Here, now, don't faint on my table," Doug said. He strode to my side with a dark bottle in his hand, flipping the porcelain swing cap off its perch. "My home brew. Best beer around. Let's get some color into your face. Want to talk about it?"

Quick shake. *No.* I wrapped my fingers around the fat, warm bottle and took a long swig. Smooth, oak-flavored, and probably way above the standard alcohol content in American beers. It hit my stomach like a hot tonic. The stars faded. I felt the warmth rush upwards.

"There's some pink!" Doug said. He hurried back to the kitchen counter then returned with bowls of chips, salsa out of a grocery jar, and gooey cheese spread. "Sorry. I'm no' much of a cook. Besides, you need something in your stomach as quick as can be, besides that beer."

"Thank you." I took another swig. "Innis

& Gunn. That's what this reminds me of." I hoped to veer away from discussing what had just happened.

"A woman who knows her Scottish-made brews!" He fetched several more beers, placed them between us, and sat down across from me. "I age mine in used whiskey barrels bought from the Jack Daniels distillery in Tennessee. Gives it the oak taste with a bit of charcoal."

"My brother makes beer. He'd love this."

"Ah hah. She has a brother. Now we're getting somewhere. Was that himself you were texting? Is everything all right?"

My stomach clenched again. I finished the beer, set it aside, and opened another one. After a long swallow I confirmed that the alcohol content in each of Doug's beers could match a James Bond double martini. I felt both shaken *and* stirred. I set the bottle down hard and looked at Doug. "Are you hoping to get me drunk so I'll talk?"

He arched a brow. "I didn't foresee that you'd drink that first bottle faster than a freshman in a beer-chugging contest."

"You're right. My bad. Not your fault."

"However, I'd love to hear anything you want to tell me. How about something a bit off the main subject, not concerning you being tracked and accused of assault by

Fidgety and Shark Eye's mysterious employer? Just tell me about this beer-making brother of yours."

Safe enough. I told him Gus was named after Groucho Marx, that he was nearly as tall as Doug with red hair that had gone almost blond from years in the desert sun. That he was a captain in the army, currently stationed in Afghanistan, and that we wanted him to take an offer to come home permanently and teach at Fort Merrill down in Georgia. "It's where all the army rangers go for their mountain training," I finished.

Listening intently, Doug said, "And who's the 'we' wanting him to do that?"

Be careful. He's looking for any careless word. I took another sip of my second beer to settle my shaking hands and uncertain stomach. "Our sister." I told him about Gabby, named for Greta Garbo, and how she was known as a pickle and relish expert. I mentioned that she owned her own restaurant in L.A. called Vin E. Garr's. The moment I said that, I chewed my tongue. There's this thing called the internet. It has search engines.

Doug propped his chin on his hand. "Isn't that the place that some crazed actor is suing about? I saw something on one of the TV gossip shows."

I stared at him. "I'd assumed you weren't gay."

"Not even close, but what's that got to do with . . ."

"I don't know any straight men who watch those shows."

"It was playing on the telly in a chicken roost. I was there tending the hens."

"A TV in a chicken house?"

"Not a 'chicken house,' a fancy roosting shed where the hens are free to come and nest as they lay their eggs. Missus Katie Dood swears by it. Says her free-range hens produce a third more eggs while watching the telly." He pointed to the stack of oatmeal cookies he'd set on the table. "Did you not notice the huge brown eggs you used?"

"Yes, they're fantastic, but . . . if those hens are watching Entertainment 7 every day, they'll lay *rotten* eggs."

"So your sister is the chef I saw on Entertainment 7? Tall redhead who threatened to throw pickle juice in the face of the next reporter who stuck a video cam in her way as she walked from her car to the restaurant?"

He kept peeling me like an onion. "Feck," I said.

His blue eyes were serious, but one corner

of his lips shifted to a smile. "I see I'm teaching you the Scots language. At least the foul and honest bits."

"You win."

He raised his beer in a toast. "I'm no' trying to beat you at a game, Tal. I'm tryin' to help you. I think it's time you tell me why those two knee-breakers at the café were huntin' for you and Eve. Do you have a plan for tomorrow? What if Fidgety and Shark Eyes wise up and back track?"

"I don't want any more confrontations on my behalf. You almost got shot." I nodded at the bandage on his knuckles. "You're hurt."

"You're a cousin of Delta's. You're family. You and Eve. If I don't try to help you, she'll n'er give me another biscuit as long as I live."

"I'm putting her at risk too."

"And how could that be? Look, if there's trouble that could spread to Delta, you need to tell me. It's only fair."

I have to trust him. I want to trust him.

I downed another beer.

"Here goes."

I told him the tangled story of me and Mark Anthony Mark, starting with me at age twenty-three, moving to New York to prove I could make it without Gabby and

Gus's help then struggling to pay for culinary school. I had years of real-world experience — Gus, Gabby, and I grew up working in the Rodriquez's restaurants — but I wanted to show them, and myself, that I could make the grade in one of the Big Apple's finest eateries. I wanted to work for Mark Anthony Mark, a bonafide cooking genius, foodie celebrity, and icon of restaurant management.

Even though at first he barely noticed me among his many minions, my natural ability as a baker finally caught his attention. One thing led to another. I thought he was going to be my personal coach and mentor, and I was star struck.

How stupid. He only wanted my baked goods.

When I eventually earned my way inside his inner circle — his penthouse apartment, his two-story gourmet kitchen, and his bedroom with the view of Manhattan, I discovered that his charming public persona was the icing on a layer cake composed of equal parts Bully, Braggart, and All-Around Self-Centered Jerk.

"Eve is a liability to his public image," I finished. "He wants to stop the rumors that he has a daughter he's never seen — to concoct a pretty story that hides the facts. I just want him to leave us alone." I realized I'd downed a third beer. Hugging the bottle to my stomach, I asked, "Am I wrong for not telling Eve who her father is?"

"No. You're a good mam, the best." He took a deep breath. "I'm the son of a man who deserted my mother when she was barely more than a girl out of boarding school, and she killed herself not long after I was born. He died of a drug overdose before I was old enough to track him down and kill him."

"Oh, Doug. I'm so sorry."

"Eh." He started to rise. "I'm going to make coffee."

"Please, don't. Turnabout is fair play. Tell me more about yourself."

He settled back in the chair. From the look on his face, very few people asked him.

I listened for the next hour as he described a knock-about childhood in the Scottish countryside, raised by friends of the family and distant relations until his paternal grandmother learned about him and brought him to her comfortable home in Glasgow. Animals were his only trustworthy companions, which led him to become a veterinarian. He met his future wife, an American from a wealthy family, at an international polo competition in England, where he was a student assistant to the Scottish team's doctor.

They married, and he moved to America, becoming a well-paid private assistant veterinarian for a conglomerate owning race horses at an estate in central Florida. He and his wife enjoyed a glamorous lifestyle among the well-to-do of the racing crowd until Doug realized that his bosses viewed the stable of prime race horses as investments to be "maximized."

The senior doc on his team was following orders to kill third-rate race horses for the insurance pay-off. Doug blew the whistle on him and brought down the conglomerate's entire gaming division, including its bid to run a Florida casino. Lawyers for the conglomerate smeared him as a "foreign golddigger," tried to have him deported and his vet license revoked. His wife divorced him, their friends turned their backs, and he was left with a stack of bills and an aging race horse, Zanadu, which he'd rescued from sure death. Zanadu and his equine buddy, Pammy.

"That's when Delta Whittlespoon and Jay Wakefield rescued *me,*" he said. "I think they planned it together."

"Wait a minute." I downed my *fourth* beer.

"Wakefield. Why does that name sound familiar?"

"Wakefields own half the state. Very old family. Based in Asheville."

"Wakefield Department Store! And the Wakefield Hotel on Haywood Street. I remember, now."

"They own lots more besides that. I met Jay down in Florida. He owns a Thoroughbred farm there. Took my side in the troubles. Tried to help me. Gave me a long-term lease on this property and introduced me to Tom Mitternich, the preservation architect who lives up on Wild Woman Ridge."

"The one who married the actress, Cathy Deen, after she was scarred in that awful wreck?"

"Yep. Tom and I are talking about some way to bring the old Clapper bicycle village back to life."

"As a bicycle factory?"

"No, not likely that. But something." He leaned toward me abruptly, scrutinizing my face. "Why are you crying?"

I whipped a hand to my wet cheeks. Exhaustion, anxiety, four beers. "I miss my home. My childhood — before my parents died. No other place has felt like home since I was a kid." I wiped my eyes. "I cry when I drink too much. I'll try not to babble about my problems anymore, at least until the morning. Or about my psychic sense of smell."

He reached across the table and dabbed the delicate skin beneath my eyes with his fingertips. "I'm a Scotsman," he said. "I believe in leprechauns and banshees."

His touch melted my skin. "I thought those were *Irish* myths."

"You're dissing leprechauns as 'myths?' "

I laughed wearily. My eyes drooped.

He stood and cupped a hand under my elbow. "Come along. You've got a daughter and a goat waiting for you to sing them lullabies."

"Bah bah, black sheep," I sang as he led me down a hall shadowed by old wall sconces and soundtracked by the soothing hum of a central furnace somewhere. "Have you any wool? Yes sir, yes sir, three bags full . . . Why am I singing about sheep?"

"Beats the feck out of 'Three blind mice.' "

We stopped at the door to a guest room where Eve and Teasel were cuddling on a bed. One of them was snoring. Eve didn't snore. Must be the goat.

"Thank you," I said. "For rescuing us from Tagger and fighting the men Mark sent to find us."

"Thank you for trusting me. Now look, you'll stay here for a few days, all right? Promise. I'll call Delta tomorrow and tell her what's going on. She'll insist."

"No! How can she concentrate on the finals of the competition if she knows about Mark? He owns fifty percent of that show! He's one of the judges."

Doug groaned. "Ack. Okay, we'll leave that be. But you stay here. You can't get more hidden than here."

"All right." I wobbled. He held my elbow tighter. I swayed against him. "I'm not drunk," I told him. "I *don't* get drunk. I get *delicious.*"

His eyes crinkled. "Thank you for putting that thought in my head."

"How's your hand?" I reached for it boldly, brought it close to my eyes in the shadowy hall, and studied the bandage he'd put on his knuckles. "You have great hands."

"Feels much better," he said gruffly. "Now that you're holding it."

I kissed him on the cheek. Right at the corner of his mouth, close enough to taste the difference between light beard stubble and his lips. A breathless moment. He said against my ear, "I've n'er met a woman like you, and I want to know you. All about you.

All of you. I hope you'll kiss me again when you've not had anything much to drink. Will you?"

"Yes," I whispered. "I promise." I sleepwalked to a whitewashed metal bedstead where Eve and Teasel were sound asleep under a colorful wool blanket adorned with a fabulous garden of tiny felted flowers. I crawled in and hugged them both.

We are finally back home, I thought.

CHAPTER FOUR

Tal and Eve Take the Past for a Spin

Bright morning sunshine warmed my face. Eve was a snuggly human teddy bear inside my arms. A Himalayan cat named Fanny and a giant golden Maine Coon named Leo were curled next to us. Teasel was stretched out on the foot of the bed, and I felt safe for the first time in several weeks. Then I remembered what I'd said, and done, on the way to bed at five a.m.

I don't get drunk. I get delicious.

Instantly awake now, I eased out of bed, tucked Eve back in, scratched Teasel behind his horn nubbins, then realized I had a larger audience: the miniature pigs and a half-dozen dogs, including Peaches and Bebe, Doug's pit bulls, which he'd rescued from a fight ring.

The gang followed me to the bathroom and sat in the open doorway watching me. I sat with my head in my hands, trying to ignore them and think. Impossible. I looked through my fingers as the pigs snuffled my toes. Their soft, *uhka uhka* grunts earned them some petting. "Piggies like skritches? Yes, piggies like skritches."

I scratched them behind the ears. *I'm talking baby talk to pigs. I surrender. Doctor Doolittle has converted me.*

After I washed up, the gang followed me to the hall door, which stood ajar. I frowned at it. Had Doug looked in on us while we slept? Not cool, Doug. Leo rose on his hind legs, grabbed the old glass doorknob with both large paws, and pulled the door further open.

"Ahah," I said. "You open doors. I guess you're the gang leader? Is your name Peeping Tom?"

I saw a handwritten note taped to the outside of the door.

Tal,

I'm off to my usual long day in the field (and barn, and shed). Make yourself at home (cook something good and save me the leftovers). If you and Eve want to explore the old bicycle shops, there's a set of keys on the antler hook by the kitchen door. (The antlers are naturally shed during molt season; I don't shoot Bambi.) Good morning and welcome again to this home. (I promise you, even the pigs are housebroken.)

Doug (who also is housebroken).

P.S. On the table by the front door there's a spare phone of mine. Call me if any trouble comes by.

I removed the note and put it in my jeans' back pocket. Okay, yes. As a keepsake.

The Mystery of Free Wheeler

Bundled up against the morning wind coming down from the Ten Sisters, Eve and I walked up the lane beyond Doug's house, holding hands. Zanadu and Pammy ambled along the fence beside us.

"Time to text Uncle Gus," I said, pulling Doug's loner cell phone from a pocket of my jeans. It was early evening in Afghanistan. If he were out on a patrol, he'd answer later.

Eve ran to the fence. "Can you send him a picture of me with my friends?"

He'd wonder where we found pigs, a goat, equines, and woods in Brooklyn. "No, sweetie, maybe next time."

"It smells like Christmas here," Eve said.

"Lots of big cedar trees and firs. That's what you smell."

"Is Santa going to be able to find us?"

"Yes, sweetie. I promise."

"Will we get on an airplane and go to Aunt Gabby's house, like last year?"

"I don't know."

"I wouldn't mind staying here for Christmas. I like Doug. A lot." Oh, no. She was getting attached to Doug and his world.

"Let's talk about this later."

I tapped a quick message into the phone:

HI YA BIG BRO. ALL IS WELL. LOST MY PHONE. THIS IS A LOANER. SENDING YOU A PACKAGE ASAP. LUV, TAL AND EVE.

No response. He was probably on patrol. The silences always made Gabby and me nervous.

Eve and I walked on. A few minutes later, the lane broadened. The air stilled. Suddenly, I swore I could smell Mama's rosewater perfume and the buttery warmth of her apple cobbler. Good spirits had joined us.

"Oh, Mommy. Wow." Eve raced ahead of me as we rounded a curve into downtown Free Wheeler.

I stopped, gaping in wonder. The lost grandeur of Free Wheeler defied the words *factory village.* It was easy to see that spaces had been designed for bicycles and cars — or back in the earlier decades, wagons — to park in front of the buildings. The whole village fit into less than one city block. The main avenue was broad and paved in large octagonal stones now fringed in weeds. Doug had removed several large trees that had rooted in the avenue and the sidewalks, heaving up stones around the roots. The bare stumps looked weird, poking up among the pavers.

On the left was a row of small brick shops, connected to one another. On the right was a two-story brick factory building. All the windows were boarded over. Granite trim decorated the brickwork. Each building's main doorway was capped with a half-moon of stone carved with the shop's name. It was obvious that those names had honored the Clapper bicycle brands: The Asheville Flyer General Store, the Fast Hawk Hardware and Feed, the Red Rocket Infirmary, the Fleet Dasher Movie Palace, and . . . the Spinning Rose Bakery.

"Let's go look at that one," I said.

Eve darted to its boarded windows and peered through a hole in the planks. "This is so pretty!" I went over and squatted beside her, cupping my hands around my eyes. Inside the shadowy space I made out pale marble floors and a long marble counter top. Other than that, the interior was empty, dusty, and sad. But how wonderful it must have been. And could be, again. "I agree."

A bakery. I stood and stepped back, pivoting slowly, taking in everything.

Grand. What a strange word, but appropriate.

The long, two-story factory building did not look industrial, but instead, somehow, *friendly.* "Bicycles on the walls, look!" Eve shouted. She pointed upward. The building's rust-red bricks surrounded beautifully chiseled granite spacers, each about two-feet square and each decorated with a carving of a bicycle. In contrast, I studied the ruins of loading docks and the boarded-over windows on the bottom level. My heart twisted. What a forsaken, whimsical place. No, calling it a "factory" wouldn't do.

Over a pair of tall double doors at the center of the building, an arch of granite was engraved with this:

Enter The Hub of Imagination
The World of Clapper Motion Machines

The Hub. I loved that name.

Just beyond it was what appeared to be a once-whitewashed English cottage. The plaster was cracking and revealed red brick underneath, part of the roof was covered in a tarp, and the rest showed frail, tattered shingles. The empty window boxes sagged.

But over the door was a mysteriously elegant sign:

The Lubritorium

"It's a fairy house!" Eve squealed, running ahead. I followed her at a trot, feeling awkward. Tall, plus-sized women don't generally jog like graceful gazelles. Picture me: an overgrown strawberry shortcake kind of gal in Crocs with candy-striped socks showing, faded jeans with forks and spoons embroidered on the legs, my cupcake hoodie, and a pink felt cap crammed on my head with wild streamers of red hair falling out the bottom.

When I caught up with her in The Lubritorium's yard, I noticed two crumbling concrete pads out front. When we cupped our hands around our faces and peeked through cracks in the boarded windows, we saw stained concrete floors, piles of undecipherable metal junk, but on a wall dimly lit by a ray of sunshine, a hand-painted sign:

Restorative Services for Wheeled Conveyances

Bicycle Tubes Repaired, Automotive Needs Resolved

If It Rolls and Is In Need of Assistance, We can Return It To Its Original Glory.

A garage! "This is an old-fashioned gas station," I told Eve.

She kept peeking through the window boards. "Where's the Freezie machine and the video games?"

"Those weren't around, then. This was built when women were just starting to drive cars. So the gas stations were made to look like . . . like pretty little houses that girls would enjoy."

"I like it!"

"Me, too." My mind began to churn. I held up the jangling key chain from Doug's free-range antler hooks. "Let's go inside the biggest building and explore!"

She grabbed my hand, and we headed for The Hub.

The Spinning Rose

A squirrel chattered furiously at us from a perch on one of The Hub's granite window caps. I filched a pinch of muffin from my hoodie's pocket. When Doug returned from his rounds, he'd find a plate of fresh-baked blueberry and oatmeal-raisin treats waiting for him. Also a cheese quiche, yeast rolls, and fresh, whole-wheat bread. I don't know how to flirt very well, but I know how to cook. Mama said cooking is love.

"Here, sweetie." I handed the tidbit to Eve then picked her up.

She reached above us and tucked it in a crevice in the bricks. "Happy breakfast, Mr. Squirrel!"

The squirrel rushed down, took the crumb in his mouth, then hustled back up to the door cap. Eve laughed. He then scurried up the bricks to a small vent with a hole gnawed in it. He disappeared into the bricks.

What else lives inside these buildings? I eased up to The Hub's weathered double doors. First I fitted a small key into a padlock to release the chain that latched their matching bronze door pulls, and when that was open, I stuck a long, antique door key into the lock. I set Eve down. Turning it required both hands. Finally the lock gave way with a rusty, scraping *clack*.

My breath caught in my throat as I turned a screeching bronze door knob and shoved hard. The heavy door swung inward. Eve and I peered into a large, long world of high ceilings and musty woodwork. Not that I could see much of it since bicycle parts filled every available square foot around the entrance area. They even dangled from the ceiling like strange birds. "They're flying!" Eve whispered.

Dust motes sifted through beams of sunlight pouring through several windows on the far side of the building.

Good. I hated the dark. Even the dim gave me jitters. I had memories from some frightening incidents in foster care. I slowly stepped over the sill, holding Eve by the hand.

"Look at the floor," she whispered, as if we were in church.

On its pale marble background was a large mural of colorful marble chips. The scene depicted Free Wheeler — the buildings, the Ten Sisters mountains behind them. Happy adults and children rode bicycles down the avenue. Dogs galloped alongside them, bluebirds flew overhead, and a crowd of happy onlookers waved from the sidewalk.

"That must be Mr. Claptraddle," I said, pointing to a tall, smiling man who stood directly in front of the Hub's main doors. He wore a snazzy blue suit, sported a handlebar mustache, and on his head were goggles like the drivers of the earliest cars once used. Beside him, waving was a woman with red hair, a green dress, and a white apron. "What's she got in her hand?" I said aloud, bending down in the uneven light.

Eve hunkered on the dusty marble and peered along with me. "It's a flower, Mommy."

"Looks like a rose."

"She's so pretty."

Enthralled, we spent a long time studying the ornately detailed and vaguely sad mosaic. Like a pretty gravestone, it marked a life that had passed on.

"What's this, Mommy?" Eve drew her fingers over four numbers etched in one corner. "One. Nine. Three. Nine. What's that mean?"

"Nineteen thirty-nine. This picture was set in the floor in the year nineteen thirty-nine."

She tried counting on her fingertips while chewing her lower lip. For a five-year-old, she did a good job of ciphering simple addition and subtraction, but this was too much for her. "That was so long ago there aren't any numbers for it."

I smiled. "Come on. Let's explore some more."

Taking her hand again, we sidled between

rows of wheel-less bicycle bodies, piles of handlebars, and other assorted parts. Ideas tumbled through my mind. *Charming, unique, historic, sturdy. Lots of space. A good vibe.* Arlo Claptraddle had successfully manufactured and sold bicycles from this "village" hidden in the mountains. He hadn't had the benefit of online mail order, websites, email, or express shipping companies. He'd trucked his bicycles over the mountains to Asheville and shipped them from the railroad at Biltmore Village, built by the Vanderbilts at the turn of the last century. *If Arlo could run a successful business from here . . .*

I heard growls behind us.

Big, deep, throaty growls. No, not growls, *snarls.* And then came the click-clack of feet. No, not feet. Paws. Huge, running paw-feet with enormous claws, coming up the weedy sidewalk beside the weedy side street that had, once upon a time, led down the hill to many lovely Free Wheeler bungalows with gardens, family milk cows, and chicken coops, now all forest and brambles and unfound murdered bodies and cupcake-craving bears and monsters for all I knew. I hoisted Eve into my arms.

Peaches and Bebe charged past us.

I backed away, bumping into bicycle

skeletons, cold dust motes poofing around Eve and me in the gray, dim air, me feeling like Indiana Jones and the Temple of Doomed Bikers.

The pit bulls, their heads covered in scars — Doug had gotten them from a rescue organization that rehabilitated ring fighters — stopped at a tiny hole in the wide plank floor. They snuffled the hole loudly. When they looked away, a mouse popped up. When they looked back, the mouse dropped out of sight. Look away, mouse popped up. Look back, no mouse. This happened a half-dozen times.

"They're not very bright," I said. "Or else that mouse is a *genius.*"

Eve giggled.

I looked around warily. My eyes rose to the sturdy wooden ceiling. Eve went "Oh!" on a long sigh of delight. There, as if separated in a lonely castle tower to protect her from invaders, hung the most beautiful old bicycle I'd ever seen. I say 'her' because she had a downward-swooping central bar to accommodate a woman rider's skirt. Her wheels were intact, but the tire tubes were missing. Layers of dust could not hide how pretty her glossy red paint must have been. She was slender but sturdy, with graceful metal mud shields curving over the backs of her tires. Her wide handlebars curled gently, ending in crackled, dried-out remnants of what must have been beautiful leather hand-grips. Behind her white leather seat was a pretty wicker basket.

"Toto?" Eve called softly. "Are you in there?"

The crowning touch? The head of an umbrella protruded from the top of a long metal tube attached to the column of the front wheel. The handle appeared to be carved from fine wood. It was topped by a carved flower, stained a deep red shade that even decades of dust couldn't obscure.

A rose.

"This must be a Spinning Rose bicycle," I whispered. "Isn't she special?"

Eve clutched my hand hard. "I want a bicycle. I want to live here, Mommy. With you. And Doug. And Teasel and all the other animals." When I looked down at her in startled silence, she sniffed back tears, and her mouth quivered. "You told me we'd have a real house one day with a yard and a swing. There's plenty of room for a swing in Doug's yard."

"Sweetie, we're just visiting here, and . . ." Peaches and Bebe charged past us again, barking but wagging their tails. They bounded out the open front doors. "Stay right here while I go look."

I hurried to the door and craned my head to peek out. Doug's big veterinary truck rolled up the avenue. When he saw me, he tapped the horn. I called to Eve to follow me and stepped outside. My heart kicked up a notch, a big notch, as he swung down from the cab and walked toward us. He had tasted so good last night.

His expression was guarded. "What do you think? Odd old place, isn't she? A bit spooky."

"We love it."

I watched his face brighten instantly. "You wouldn't be kidding me, would you?"

"Not kidding."

" 'Tis a wistful little world. Some say haunted. Useless. What can be done with it out here in the midst of the woods?"

"Arlo was able to sell bikes from here. That couldn't have been easy back in the day. All it takes is passion and a plan."

He smiled widely. Eve ran up to him. "We saw a Spinning Rose!"

"Did you now? She's the most beautiful bike he made, I say. She's named for Rose, his wife." When he said 'wife' he used careful emphasis and gave me a meaningful glance. Wife in name only? Interesting.

"Is she the redhead in the mural?" I asked.

"Hmmm uh."

I pointed toward the Spinning Rose bakery shop. "And a baker?"

"That's what they say. Delta believes she was kin to Mary Eve Nettie, like about half of everyone in Jefferson County. I see she's caught your fancy."

"A redhead who baked? You bet! You and Jay Wakefield and Tom Mitternich have to come up with a plan for this village. It's got —" I sifted the air with my hands, searching for the right words — "a deep heart."

He studied me in a way that made my knees weak. Eve patted his hand, breaking the spell. "Doug?"

"Yes, Miss?"

"Have you ever thought of putting a swing in your front yard?"

"No, but I think that's a fine idea!"

Oh, no, this was getting *so* involved. I cleared my throat. "Is anything wrong? I mean, you're coming here during the middle of a work day."

He arched a brow at my brusque attitude. "As a matter of fact, I dropped by to fetch you and Eve, if you want to go. Jay Wakefield's flying in for lunch at the café, and he wants to meet you."

"You . . . told him about Eve and me?"

"No, Cleo did."

I'll shove her head in an oven.

"You're turning fire-red. Delta told her to do it."

I was stunned. "Cleo called Delta? Why?"

"I'm not sure. Delta's always scheming to bring folks together. Also, she says everything's gone frantic in New York, and Cathy's ordered her to get more rest. No more long-distance baking. You're to be given full run of the kitchen, and she'll be forever grateful if you'd do her the honor of making the daily biscuits until she comes home in a week or two. Full pay. Will you accept?"

"We really should move on. My sister in California would be happy to see us." Yes, make our way west to Gabby's condo in California. Allow Eve the time to forget about Doug, Teasel, and front yard swings and magical vintage bicycles. Let me forget, too.

"Mommy," Eve said wistfully. Her eyes were wide and hopeful. "Santa can't find us if we're driving in the car. There's no chimney to come down."

"Stay here through the holidays," Doug urged. "We'll go over to a Christmas tree farm near Turtleville and pick out whatever tree you like best. Can you make some decorations? I have not a one. Unless you'd like to hang bicycle parts and horseshoes."

"Mommy makes gingerbread people to hang on Christmas trees!"

This was quicksand. I felt myself sinking. He added quietly, "Stay, and give me a chance to help you work things out."

I grasped one remaining lifeline. A thorny one. "What about Cleo? She can't be happy about me getting Delta's blessing."

"Delta's the boss. Someone's got to make the biscuits. Cleo knows that." He paused. "Besides, she only shoots ceiling fans, not cousins."

Done. I was sunk.

And strangely elated about that fact.

The Dark Wizard of Wakefield Arrives

Doug was not kidding. Jay Wakefield *flew* in from Asheville via his own two-seater helicopter. He set it down in the pasture by the café, just far enough from two inflated snowmen to make them bob wildly but not lift off like unleashed balloons. Several angus beef cows shook their black heads at him as he strode across the field toward Doug and me. He whipped off dark sunglasses and tucked them into a brown leather bomber jacket. Jay had played tight end for the UNC Tar Heels, where Wakefields funded several scholarships in the school of business; now, in his mid-thirties, he still had beefy shoulders and lean hips. His face was roughly handsome, the jaw too thick, the nose crooked, with a high forehead and deep gray eyes. His black hair was cut crisply and short. He looked like a hit man, not the heir to one of the state's most powerful dynasties. The snowmen bowed and straightened, bowed and straightened.

Gabby would eat him up with a drizzle of balsamic vinaigrette and a side of her secret-recipe hot jalapeno relish. As a kid, she'd had a huge crush on him. Everyone knew it, though she'd never admit that. Now he had all the right spices for her grown-up tastes, as well: a jock's swagger, a gangster's attitude, and a GQ model's haircut.

He stopped on the other side of the fence, his western boots sinking into mushy brown grass. The sky had gone from bright blue to a low ceiling of slate-gray snow clouds. So had Wakefield's day, apparently. "Late," he grunted as he grabbed Doug's hand in a hearty shake. "Sorry. Three-hour planning session on the Land of the Sky project. Biggest mixed-use development in the history of the state. Community watchdog groups are up in arms. Zoning issues. Fussy old hippies and tree-hugging save-the-wildflower activists."

Instantly I disliked him. Gus and Gabby told me how Mama had led a community group against developers who wanted to raze some of Asheville's wonderful old buildings. Without people like her, the city would be modern and generic now.

As Doug made introductions, Jay palmed my hand in a surprisingly gentle squeeze. "So you're the biscuit witch. Do you specialize in black magic or white magic?"

"Depends on what the spell calls for. Angel Food or Devil's Food."

"What do you call your sister? I've seen the footage of her threatening reporters with pickle brine."

"Don't tell me you've forgotten her name."

"Never. I mean, her 'nom de cuisine.' If you're the biscuit witch, then what is she?"

"She still goes by 'the Pickle Queen.' "

He tilted his head and looked upward, as if imprinting Gabby's whimsical title on his deepest memories. "I'm glad. Good branding potential. The Pickle Queen."

"I'm sure she thinks you've forgotten her," I said through gritted teeth. "Forgotten all of us, in fact."

"I never turned my back on the three of you. You left the state. Decided you wanted nothing to do with an evil Wakefield."

"We were kids. We had no choice."

"Neither did I." The scowl growing in his rugged expression smoothed into an unsettling poker face. "I've kept track. Greta Garbo MacBride. Thirty-one. Six-feet tall. Interned in the kitchen at the French Laundry in Napa Valley before hooking up with John Michael Michael to open a restaurant . . ."

"She didn't 'hook up' with him. It was a business partnership. He liked her pickles."

"I'm not trying to insult you or her. Just being blunt. Doug warned you about that, didn't he?"

Doug looked angry. "I told her you're an arrogant bastard at first glance."

Jay nodded to him and smiled. "And at a second glance, too." Then, turning to me, he said, "How's Gus? Still wasting his life in the army? What? Fifteen years now?"

He's researched us. Why?

"What's his thing, Tal? His culinary thing. You're the baker, your sister's the pickler. What was it your mother nicknamed him? Wait, I remember. 'The Kitchen Charmer.' Doesn't he have a specialty?"

"Beer. He makes great beer."

"Good. We'll have to think of a better brand persona for him. The Brew Master. The Suds Sultan. We'll work on it."

Doug cut the air with a sharp gesture. "What's this about?"

"I'm almost done, my friend. Tal, trust me, I respect your family. You've run a respected little bakery. Gabby's got what it takes to run a top-dollar restaurant if she weren't saddled with the wrong partner. And I've seen Gus's army records. He makes friends with tribal leaders by cooking them dinner. Amazing. Together, the three of you could be worth my investment. I want to hire you to set up a restaurant in Free Wheeler. What would it take? I know you're barely making a living in New York and Gabby's just lost everything, plus Gus makes squat as an army officer. What have you got to lose?"

I clenched my fists. "You put it such a charming way."

Doug stepped slightly in front of me. His jaw flexed. "You're my friend, Jay, and I know you've not got much diplomacy about you, but you're about to find yourself arse backwards on the grass with an angus heifer trying to have her way with you."

"I apologize, Doc. You're right." To me he said, vaguely sincere and completely unfazed by our darkening mood, "My bedside manner went to hell a lot of years ago. I used it all up sitting by bedsides. I apologize. Really."

"What makes you suddenly decide to offer three strangers a business to run?" I asked.

"You'll never be strangers to me." He pivoted toward Doug. "Gus and I are the same age. I used to escape from my grandfather's offices in Asheville every afternoon and go to the MacBrides' diner on Lexington. I was pals with Gus, Gabs and baby Tal. Their parents made me feel at home. I liked it." He delivered that startling news with a cast-off nonchalance that hid any deeper emotions. He paused. "Gabs and I were close. Still are."

That sounded mysterious. "Wait a second. You were asking me questions about her as if you didn't know much."

"I wanted to see how much you'd trust me. And to confirm that my current information is correct."

Doug said grimly, "You've heard of Machiavelli? He was a Wakefield."

Jay laughed and nodded. He pulled a thick envelope from an inside pocket of his jacket. "As I said, I see the potential in the MacBride franchise. I'm picturing Free Wheeler as a lifestyle destination property — recreate the bicycle paths, put in a museum of the ol' Clapper trappers or whatever they were called, plus a large inn, shops, a pub, a restaurant, hiking trails, a small conference center — all spread out artfully and intimately throughout the bee-u-tee-ful six hundred acres that encompass Free Wheeler. Combined with the folksy allure of the Crossroads community and Tom Mitternich's ideas for developing his vineyard into a full-fledged winery . . . let's put it this way: I'd call it "Little Napa Valley of the Appalachians," and promote it as an anchor for development of these isolated communities — bringing jobs and opportunities but not destroying the independence and serenity around here."

He nodded to Doug. "It would include that no-kill pet shelter and wildlife rehab sanctuary we've discussed."

Doug was not smiling. "You'd destroy what makes it special. Turn it into a gawker's resort, no better than a theme park. Does Tom know about this?"

"No, and why should he? Tom is a consultant; he doesn't make decisions for me. He'll either agree, or I'll hire someone new. He swiveled his wolfish stare to me: "You MacBrides have the Appalachian street cred to be taken seriously up here." He held out the envelope to Doug and me. "Just take a look at the proposal."

After a tense moment, Doug shook his head. "I'm not having any part of this."

"That's not fair, Doc. You should at least look at the plan. Tal?"

I took the envelope. "I agree with Doug, but I have a duty to tell Gabby and Gus what you're offering them." I cast a quick *forgive me* glance at Doug. He gave a slight nod.

Jay tilted his head, studying the interaction. "She's a keeper, Doug."

"Back off," Doug growled.

"I still like you, Tal. When you were a little girl, I'm guessing three years old, your mother let you play with cookie dough every day. You'd put strange things in it like grapes and pimentos, then you'd pat your concoctions into little cakes and share them with anyone brave enough to sample raw dough with strange lumps in it. I ate one once just to see you smile." He paused, arching a brow. "I was sick that night."

A strong scent-memory rose in my mind. Pepsi Cola and ketchup. He was the PC and Ketchup Boy. There had been something sweet but sad about him.

He held out a hand to me. "You'll read the proposal and share it with Gus and Gabs. Deal?"

Deal. *Gabs.* She'd slice him like a gherkin if he called her that now. What had gone on between them as kids? And had there been something between them in the two decades since? I shook his hand but didn't let go immediately. "Are you really a witch?" he asked, trying and failing to sound completely bemused. "What are you doing?"

"I'm deciding what you smell like. Not your aftershave or cologne or laundry detergent. You. Your spiritual scent."

"Doug, does she still make raw cookies with unnatural ingredients in them? I'm not sure she's safe."

Doug scowled at him. "You'll get no sympathy from me."

I released his hand. *He's changed. That gentle boy is barely there.* "You smell like something that's learned to grow in the dark. Something buried. Potatoes. And mushrooms."

He frowned but quipped, "Not truffles? Wakefields are the truffles of the root fungi world."

Still frowning, he pivoted toward Doug. "We'll work this out, Doc. You love Free Wheeler, and you've taken care of it. I respect that. But I'm going to turn it into an asset instead of a peculiar obsession that my great-grandfather chained to my family's name."

He nodded his goodbyes to us then strode back to his helicopter.

"That was his idea of 'doing lunch?' " I asked, dazed.

"He lives on protein bars and bourbon. The stupid, greedy bastard."

"I'm sorry if it sounded like I'm encouraging his plan. I'm not."

Doug faced me, looking conflicted. "I don't like what he's springing on us. But . . . I like the idea of you staying around here for good."

The words enclosed us in a cocoon. We stood there, just looking into each other's eyes without speaking. Finally, the loud whir of Jay Wakefield's helicopter broke the spell.

After it disappeared through a gap in the mountains, I opened the envelope. Doug and I read the enclosed pages quickly.

Jay would fund all costs to turn Free Wheeler into the centerpiece of a To-Be-Named-Later "mountain village." He offered Doug a long-term contract as head of a veterinary complex including a wildlife rehab center and "management of scenic wildlife populations." He offered me, Gabby, and Gus a five-year contract to design, implement, and manage "upscale restaurant and food services to be agreed upon in negotiations." In return we'd get generous salaries, benefits, and a small share in any profits. But he'd own it all.

"He'd be our employer not our partner," I said. "But . . . Gabby and I used to dream about running a restaurant together — and getting Gus to come home and run it with us. Maybe this is the only way that can happen."

Doug took a step back, hands on hips, head down, thinking hard. Then, "I'd hoped to buy the property one day. At least the house, the barn, and a few acres besides. My ancestors were farmers and shepherds. They loved their land but lost it time and again to politics and rich men. I have that love of the soil in me and that love of the animals that share the land and their lives with us. I came to this country for love of a woman and the dream of having what my ancestors could n'er keep — a home and independence. The first was misguided, but the second was burned into my blood. I'll not work for Jay or for anyone else but myself. And I'll not stand by and watch quietly as he turns a legacy and a paradise into a fecking silly playground where the wild beasts are scenic and only those people with plenty o' cash can visit. I'll fight him tooth and nail." He took a huge breath and dropped his hands to his sides. "But I understand what an opportunity like this means for you and your kin. I'll not hold it against you if you take the deal."

That was the exact moment I fell in love with him.

"I'll tell Gus and Gabby about this offer," I said quietly. "But I'll also tell them to count me out. I remember something Delta wrote to us when we were teenagers. She said, 'People are like dough. Some are too soft, some are too stiff, some are just waiting to rise to the occasion, and some will fall flat no matter how much you try to lighten them up.' " I held up the paperwork. "You've got the makings of a great biscuit, Doug Firth."

I tore the pages into small bits and handed him half of them. We tossed the offer into the mountain breeze. He stepped toward me, a gleam in his eyes like a blue flame. "I'm going to take you up on that promise of another kiss."

I reached for him and him for me. My body tingled, and the scent of papaya rose in my brain. In my psychic recipe book, "papaya brain" is one teaspoon away from a public orgasm.

The long, loud, screeching honk of an air

horn blasted the wonderful moment to pieces.

"It's eleven a.m.!" Cleo bellowed from the veranda of the gonzo Christmas extravaganza otherwise known as The Crossroads Café. She shook the air horn at me. "Your first batch of biscuits should be ready for the oven by now!"

I waved. Suddenly the Devil's Food possessed me, and the wave turned into the middle-finger-only variety.

"I couldn't agree more," Doug said.

Tal Sets Up a Care Package

At one point during lunch I looked up from my dough to find Brittany, Danielle, and Jenny staring at me and biting their smiles. They fled the kitchen quickly. I looked around for clues and found Cleo's glare. "If you keep rubbing that dough that way, it's gonna ask you out on a date. Doc'll be jealous."

She knew. Everyone knew. Doug and I were an item, less than twenty-four hours after we'd met. My thoughts swirled from heated feelings for him to Jay Wakefield's offer and back again. My life, and Eve's, had turned completely upside down, and yet . . . it felt exciting. I should be terrified. With my track record? Absolutely.

Gus's text came through that afternoon as I prepped the first of the biscuit dough for the dinner menu. Doug was back at work, answering his routine vet calls. Eve and Teasel were outside chasing squirrels under the oaks.

LONG DAY. GOOD TO HEAR FROM YOU. SEND SOME HAPPY TEETH.

"Happy teeth," I said aloud, frowning at Doug's spare phone.

"Beg pardon?" Arnold asked. He was elbow-deep in raw chicken parts, battering them in buttermilk and cornmeal.

"My brother is texting from Afghanistan. When he asks for 'happy teeth' he's had a rough time on patrol. He wants us to send pictures of our smiles." I clapped a flour-dusted hand to my forehead. "And I've got to put together his care package today! I almost forgot! It's three weeks until Christmas, and we always send more goodies during the holidays."

"What kind of care package?" Bubba asked from the grill station. He stopped scrubbing the grill to wipe his hands on his apron. "Toothpaste and such? We've got all sorts of toiletries in the store."

"No, we send him food. Cookies, fudge,

pies, pickles, jam — anything that preserves well enough to survive the trip. He likes to share with his soldiers. Plus he takes some of it to the locals. Offering food is a powerful bonding ritual. He's built up trust with men who won't talk to any other Americans."

"Then let's get started on that package." Bubba disappeared into the back storage area and returned with a huge, heavy-duty box. "We do a fair amount of shipping to our long-distance customers. We can pack a feast in this thing."

"I'll get the vacuum bagger," said Arnold. "We'll seal everything up in air-tight pouches."

Jenny looked up from cleaning heads of cabbage for cole slaw. "Would Gus like some home-canned produce? We've got a pantry full. Tomato and okra stew, pole beans, summer squash . . ."

"You guys are wonderful." I put a dusty hand to my throat. "Thank you."

Bubba pulled a cell phone out of the overalls he wore with an Atlanta Braves jersey. A few clicks later, he held it out. I looked at a freckled twenty-something in a marine uniform. "Cleo and me have a son who served in Iraq." He paused, his throat working. "Lost a leg. He's been home for a year now. Somewhere out west. Gambling and doing who-knows-what. We've tried everything to get him back here, but he says he doesn't want his family and old friends treating him like a cripple."

"I'm so sorry, Bubba." *No wonder Cleo is in a bad mood all the time.*

Bubba scrubbed a hand under one eye, leaving a smear of grill grease. He cleared his throat and put the phone away. He patted the enormous box. "Let's fill this up with goodness."

Tal and Eve Show Some Happy Teeth

Five p.m. The dough for the dinner biscuits was ready to bake, and Gus's care package was nearly full. Swaddled in Styrofoam and bubble wrap were jars of soup, okra, beans, and stewed apples from an orchard near Turtlesville. Also local cheeses, a crockery jar full of fresh butter, jams made from the berries at Rainbow Goddess Farm, and a large bag of stone-ground grits.

And then there were the baked goods. Everyone had pitched in, under my direction, to make piles of decorated Christmas cookies. Last but not least, I baked two-dozen biscuits for him. Vacuum sealed and carefully protected in their own small box, they had a decent chance of arriving in edible condition.

Bubba and Arnold hoisted the giant box onto a scale in the back room. "Forty-two pounds," Bubba called. "I'll seal this up and have it ready for the mail in the morning."

It would cost a small fortune to ship. "Can you deduct the shipping cost from my salary for today?"

"I could, but that wouldn't be how family treats family. Delta would skin me alive. Nope, this one's on the house."

I carried a smaller box to the back. It, too, was packed with cookies and biscuits. "Do you have a mailing address for your son?"

Bubba looked stricken. "Yeah, I do. Not that he answers when we write to him."

"Will you send this to him? Sometimes a taste of home does more good than we expect."

He smiled. "You sound just like Delta." He took the box gently. "Thanks. And listen . . . whatever's going on between you and Doug, lemme tell you: he's a good man. We've seen him handle terrible situations — sad ones with animals that are hurt too bad to save; their owners in hysterics. He's got a calmness and a kindness about him that soothes people as well as animals." Bubba nodded at the box of cookies for his and Cleo's son. "Sort of the way you work your biscuit magic."

"I like him," I said. "I like him a lot."

"I'm rooting for you two."

I smiled at him, suddenly misty-eyed. I scrubbed the dampness with the hem of my apron. "Back to work before Cleo gets the air horn out again."

He laughed.

I called Eve in from the yard. She was pink, sweaty, laughing, and covered in dirt. So was Teasel — except for the pink part. "We were jumping logs," she explained. I had never seen her look so happy.

I brushed her hair, took off my hairnet, then posed her in front of the work counters and stoves. Pretty generic kitchen stuff. Gus might think we were visiting a friend's kitchen in Brooklyn.

"I'll be your photographer," Arnold volunteered.

I knelt by Eve. We draped our arms around each other's shoulders, held up a couple of cookies, and grinned widely for the camera. Arnold snapped several pictures before we agreed on the one with the happiest teeth.

I had just finished texting that one to Gus when Eve tugged on my apron. I looked down to find her pondering me solemnly. "My teeth are really, really happy here. Can we stay with Doug and not go back to

Brooklyn?"

I took her hand. We went out on the kitchen porch and sat on the steps. I chose my words as if each one was a crucial dab of icing on an edible portrait of the Mona Lisa. *We have lots of friends in New York, sweetie. Wouldn't you miss your classmates? Mommy and Doug just met. We'd have to get to know Doug for months and months before . . .*

"He makes you smile," she countered. "And he likes your biscuits."

Good points.

"I hear your heart when you look at him."

I had told her how babies in the womb hear something no one else in the world can share: their mothers' heartbeats.

"Do you, sweetie?"

"Hmmm uh. And I hear Doug's heart, too."

My throat closed with the sweetness of her ideas. I was still hunting for words when a truck rumbled down the lane. Macy waved at us and leaned out the window as she pulled alongside. "Doc's okay, but he could use a little TLC. A llama kicked him in the head."

We climbed in her truck and headed for Rainbow Goddess Farm.

Doug and the Llamas. Yes, They Spit

His name was Liberace, because every male animal at Rainbow Goddess was named after a famous gay man. I couldn't figure out the symbolism, since the boys were all there as breeding studs, not to act like girlfriends with testicles. Anyhow, the shaggy llama bastard bit me on the shoulder as I knelt beside his special lady, Hillary, as in Clinton. I was tying off the last suture on a nasty shoulder wound she'd gotten from the sharp branch of a fallen tree. It must've seemed to Liberace that I was taking liberties with her and that she was fallin' under my manly Celtic spell since she kept curling her head around to sweetly nibble the sleeve of my jacket.

So Liberace, the jealous bastard, emitted a deep, snorting, growlish sound then bit me hard atop my left collarbone. It hurt like a "sumbitch," as Pike Whittlespoon taught me to say during his Saturday-night poker games, even though I was wearing a heavy coat over a thick wool shirt. As I leaned back to yell at him, Liberace reared and flung out a front hoof. Clipped me right between the eyes.

I fell back amidst the shouts of Alberta and several o' her women helpers who murmured a prayer or two as I passed out.

They might have been praying that my head hadn't hurt Liberace's hooves. I blacked out when I hit the winter-hardened ground of the barn yard.

I came to right away, unfortunately. My ears picked up a sloshy *ker-tooey* noise the instant before a stinking stream of llama spit hit me in the face. Liberace glared down at me, his lips working and his ears pinned back. He shoulda just stomped me and been done with it. But no, he had to spit. The fecker.

All in all, there was no good reason for me to do more than just lay there and squall every filthy curse I knew. But, being a gentleman, I said only, "Be damned, you fecking beastie," and sat up, swaying a bit, while Alberta and her crew grabbed Liberace by his halter and tugged him out of fightin' range. Protectin' him from me, I guess.

My ears rang, and I watched stars twirl in front of my eyes. "I'm just stunned a bit," I protested, as Alberta began dabbing my face with a towelette I'd used to wipe my hands after wiping pus off Hillary's wound. Adding insult to injury, you could say.

"Get my kit," she called to one of the women. As a trained medic, she owned some basic exam gear. I want to keep a check on your eyes in case they start to dilate. We should take you over to the clinic at Turtleville, Doc. You're getting a knot on your head."

"I've a hard head, and it has been rattled far worse in the boxing ring. I'll just go some place far away from Liberace and sit for a while, ponderin' a new career. Maybe I'll take up skinning llamas for a living."

She helped me up. I wobbled a mite on the way to the nearest llama-free zone. "Yep, I'm going to check your eyes," she confirmed.

The next thing I knew, Alberta was sending Macy to fetch Tal. The consensus? That I shouldn't be allowed to drive home. As I leaned back on an old lounge chair Lucy set out for me in her wool-working shed, I thought of the smelly, knot-headed sight I'd make to Tal. I began scrubbing my face no matter how much that hurt.

This is what love is. When nothing matters except cleaning off the llama spit before your lady sees you.

Tal Goes Over the Rainbow

Trust your inner woman and the girl she used to be, Macy sang at the top of her lungs, accompanying herself on her iPod-connected radio. She wailed loudly to the background of fiddles, guitars, and the exotic drumming of an African drum. *Listen to your female soul and not the heart men want to steal. Respect your body and your mind, not just your sex appeal . . . And walk the path of power 'til you find the you that's real.*

Macy clicked the iPod, and the music stopped.

Eve looked at me wide-eyed, her hands over her ears.

"That's our music!" Macy explained as she steered her truck up a winding dirt road among high mountain pastures rimmed in deep forest. She glanced across me to smile at Eve. "Sorry I turned it up too loud, honey!"

"That's okay, ma'am," Eve shouted. "What'd you say?"

"That's mine and Alberta's 'folkgrass' band. We're The Log Splitter Girls."

I massaged Eve's ears. "I get the feeling men aren't welcome at your farm?"

"Not generally, though Tom Mitternich has become a good pal, and the Doc is a great guy. It's just that we take in a lot of women who need to break their dependency on men — the bad ones, but the good ones, too — so they can stand up for themselves and their kids. Even a good man may not be around to take care of things forever. So we teach self-sufficiency. I don't mean we teach them how to make a living on a farm — the farm work is only a way to show them how they can learn new skills and make a new life."

"So Doug . . . Doctor Firth . . . keeps his distance from them? What happens if he's swarmed by grateful women who recognize a diamond after settling for a lifetime of rocks?"

"Oh, a few have tried to cozy up to him. By nature he's drawn to the hurt, the weak, and the homeless. But we warned him on his first visit that he'd need to keep it in his pants. He's been tempted, he admits that, but he is a morally substantial Person of the Opposite Gender."

Does Doug see Eve and I as a pair of needy souls like his scarred pit bulls and his rescued horse? Are we fixer-uppers like the buildings in Free Wheeler?

"What does Doug have in his pants?" Eve whispered to me.

"Sssh, Macy's just making a joke."

Macy slapped her forehead. "Sorry. We're very open about sexuality around the women and their kids. We believe in education, awareness, and forthright discussion. But I mean no disrespect toward your way of raising your child. I'm not saying her natural curiosity is being repressed just . . . oops."

She made me feel like a *primster* — which, in fact, is what Gabby sometimes called me.

I snorted. "Sweetie, tell Macy about the cake I made for the baby shower that time. You know, the one the baby's mother wanted done made a very special way, and you happened to come into my kitchen at the shop and saw it on the decorating table, and I explained to you what it was about?"

Eve bounced on the seat. She loved the story of that bizarre cake. "It was a big pink tummy of the mommy's, and it had part of her legs on it, too, and a baby was coming out from between them. Because a baby falls out of a woman's vagina when it's born, and vaginas are made of pink fondant with purple sprinkles."

Macy cracked up. "Purple sprinkles?"

"We weren't going for anatomically correct," I said. *But back to the subject of Doug.* "Doctor Firth doesn't strike me as the kind of man who is lonely . . ." I was going to be extremely euphemistic around my daughter regarding the Future Daddy she had zeroed in on . . . "he has a lot of . . . *friends,* I expect."

Macy cut her eyes at me. "He's had a respectable share. Delta and Cathy Mitternich are always matchmaking for him. But for one thing, he works ten, twelve hours a day minimum, driving all over Jefferson County, three hundred and sixty-five days a year, plus emergencies at night. Not many women can deal with that schedule. Plus he's skittish about commit . . ."

I thumbed the air in Eve's direction. Macy mouthed 'Oh, sorry,' then finished, "He has high standards."

"Good for him," I chirped, and distracted Eve by pointing at the well-tended and art-fully designed herb-and-vegetable gardens that began rolling by on either side of the driveway to Rainbow Goddess Farm. Old wheelbarrows made potting beds for winter cabbage, whirligigs pirouetted in the brisk mountain breeze, and birdhouses on tall posts stood like pretty sentinels among the sleeping rows where next year's crops would grow. It was all so fundamentally pure and earthy, a sweet setting where folk-art fairies might spring out from behind the last of the fall pumpkins, flitting on wings cut from vintage auto tags and pimped out in rhine-stones.

"What's that stone lady doing, Mommy?"

The eight-foot statue rose from a knee-high cluster of rosemary shrubs. Her face was turned heavenward and her chunky, naked body seemed to relish the open air. One hand was lifted toward the sky.

The other was between her thighs.

Beside me, Macy tried not to laugh. She tried so hard that the effort turned into a fit of hiccups.

"The stone lady is just keeping her fondant warm," I told Eve.

Inside Lucy's Spinning World

Lucy wouldn't touch a man, not for any reason, not even me, who had worked hard to become her trusted friend and be a good representative of the manly gender. I had no self-serving designs on her — not that small, heavily medicated blondes who armor themselves in granny dresses with overalls underneath aren't quite fine by me, but my taste runs to big, curvy women with manes of red hair and freckles. A woman who wears pink but doesn't look girly in it, who can sweet talk biscuits, and who carries a gun. A woman who likes bears, sheep, goats, pigs, and children. A woman who likes *me* and isn't shy about kissing me.

Tal. I couldn't have described Miss Perfect before I met her. When I laid eyes on Tal, I just knew. *There she is. My perfect woman.*

"Here comes another one," Lucy said. She finished wrapping ice cubes in one of her hand-knitted cotton towels, which are soft and fluffy. She leaned over the main work table in her wool shop, which is so full of dangling yarns, unspun wood, and whole fleeces that it feels like the inside of a wooly uterus, and she put the homemade ice pack on an old tin cookie sheet she used for laying out sections of carded wool, and then she gave it a push. The cookie sheet skittered across the dye-stained table, straight into my waiting hand.

"You're certain you n'er played sports?" I asked. "Bowling? Skeeball? Shooting craps? How about that batty Scandinavian game where they shove round rocks across the ice?"

" 'Curling,' " she supplied. She used to be a school teacher. *Teacher of the Year* for North Carolina before the rape, in fact. She knew interesting facts about many things. The only thing she didn't know? How to trust men again. She smiled as she backed away.

We heard footsteps on the wooden porch outside. The screen door banged open then the plank one, and in strode Macy, followed by Tal and Eve.

Tal took one look at the bump on my forehead and rushed forward. She knelt down on one knee beside my chair and studied me as if my being hurt was more upsetting than she'd expected.

Eve tiptoed up beside her, gazing at me in worried awe. "Are you growing a unicorn horn?" she asked tearfully.

It was worth getting kicked in the face by a llama.

I made a big to-do of feeling fine, though my head hurt like a sumbitch. Alberta refused to let me go home for at least an hour, so I lay back in the lounge chair with a fresh icepack on my forehead and my eyes shut. Listening to Tal's voice was good medicine.

"This is called 'roving?' " she asked Lucy.

"Yes," Lucy answered. "It's wool that's been cleaned and carded then arranged into these fat braids. I either dye them or use them in their natural color. Then I spin them into yarn."

Eve clapped her hands. "Can we watch?"

"Certainly!"

Lucy described how the wheel worked and what its various parts were called. I heard the whir as it spun and the rhythmic clicking as she worked the treadle with her feet. She let Eve give it a try, producing lots of "Look, look, Mommy!" and "Just like a spider!" as fluffs of wool turned into snuggly wound yarn. From there they went to the carding machine, where Eve tried her hand at placing bits of colorful wool on its toothy drum as Lucy turned it with a hand crank.

Tal began to sing.

"Rollin', uh huh, rollin', uh huh, rollin' on the carder," she sang like Tina Turner's *Proud Mary*. "Big drum thingie keeps on turning, proud Eve-ee keeps on . . . learnin'. Rollin', rollin', rollin' on Lucy's-wool-carding-roller-thingie."

I smiled. Pure honey filled my sore bones. I dozed.

Someone removed my ice pack. Tal's warm fingertips touched my forehead. I looked up sleepily into her beautiful green eyes and Alberta's stern hazel ones.

"He's not dead. He's just napping." Alberta grunted. "Okay. You're free to go, Doc. Home, that is. You better take it easy the rest of the day." She looked at Tal. "You check on him every couple of hours, awright? Make sure he's not cross-eyed. Get him to count your fingers. If he acts confused or his vision's blurry, call nine-one-one."

She nodded.

I sat up, flexing my sore shoulder. My head ached, but there was no dizziness. "Good as new," I announced. I squinted up at Tal. "How's the bump look?"

"Not bad," she said carefully.

Alberta snorted. "It looks like you're growing a second head."

"Ah, if only we still had good ol' fashioned carnivals. I could sign on as a sideshow freak. Go on tour."

Eve darted between Tal and Alberta. Her teary expression returned. "You're not leaving, are you, Doug?"

Tal patted her back. "He's just kidding, sweetie."

I felt like a rat for upsetting her. *Change the subject.* I sniffed the air. "What's that aroma? Do I smell . . ." I pointed at the yellow knit cap she wore. "Bananas?"

Her smile returned. "Yes!" She tugged the cap's earflaps, which lead to long braids of yellow yarn. "It's a monkey poop hat! Lucy made it for me last night!"

"Lucy dyed the yarn with food coloring," Tal explained, studying me with a glow in her eyes. "She scented the dye with banana extract."

"She's a yarn fairy!" Eve proclaimed.

I grinned. "I believe you're right, Miss Monkey Poop Hat. She knows exactly what to knit for a person. It's a magical talent."

Lucy shook her head. "It's what I'm best at. It's the way I talk to people, now.

Through the yarn."

Alberta arched a brow. "She knitted Macy a lavender lace shawl with a hummingbird pattern. But she knitted *me* a thick gray scarf with a cable pattern that looks like snakes climbing a fence."

Dead on, I thought.

"They're vines," Lucy corrected. "Strong and protective." She went to a large plastic tub on one of her work tables. "Tal, I want to pick out something for your brother. A Christmas present. To include in the care package."

Tal smiled. "That would be great."

"Do you have a picture of him?"

"On my cell phone, but . . ." She'd retrieved her cell phone from the car but was wary about turning it on. She looked at me. "Should I take the chance?"

"No, I don't think so."

"I can handle this," Alberta said. She jerked a thumb toward the outdoors. "Our survivalist bunker. It has metal walls."

Tal Is Given a Scarf for Gus

Lucy and I stood under a bare lightbulb in the underground bunker. "It feels as if we're on a secret mission," I said.

"I like it here." She touched a large woven satchel she carried with her everywhere. "I

157

have my knitting. I could be happy down here, alone."

I scrolled through my photos. "Here's my favorite." I handed the phone to her. Call me Ms. Machiavelli for selecting this particular picture of Gus.

Somewhere in the stark high mountains of Afghanistan, he sat cross-legged on the ground in front of a grill and a hot pile of coals. On the grill sat a large pan of beautiful, golden, southern-style cornbread. He was dressed in his desert camo but wore a traditional Afghan hat and fringed scarf. One hand was posed to slide a spatula under a triangle he'd carved from the bread. He gazed straight into the camera with a somber smile, his face handsome, square-jawed, and ruddy from the sun and wind. The hat hid his bleached crew cut and shadowed his green eyes. Combined with the traditional hat and scarf, the aura he gave off was mysterious and bluntly masculine.

Around him, hunkered on both sides, were smiling Afghani children. In the background stood several mothers, hidden inside burquas and scarves.

"He goes into secluded villages," I told Lucy, "and he cooks for the people. He speaks *Dari* well enough to communicate a little, plus there's always a translator with his patrol, but *food* is the main language. The villagers gave him the hat and scarf as thanks."

Lucy was so still I could barely see her chest rise and fall. She seemed hypnotized. "The hat is a *pakol*. It's made of wool. It's very baggy until you put it on and roll up the sides. Then it looks a little like a beret with a fat rim. The scarf is a *dismaal*. Thin, probably made of cotton. Woven on looms. The Afghans are exquisite weavers. Especially the women. Afghan rugs are classics."

She touched the photo gently. It appeared she was stroking the pakol and dismaal; as if she could feel the fibers through cyberspace. But then she said, "He's a Wensleydale."

"Is that good?"

"Yes. It's a breed of sheep. In fact, it's the sheep you saw yesterday."

"Ah. So . . . you're saying Gus reminds you of blue-faced sheep with corkscrew curls?"

She smiled slightly, more wistful than happy. She never took her eyes off his photo. "He's a strong fiber, almost coarse compared to the delicate wools, and with a long draft."

I could have inserted a good crack about

Gus appreciating her estimate of his draft, but joking about men was not a good idea. "Draft? You mean, as in what you told us about working with different lengths of hair, depending on the breed of the sheep?"

"Uhmm huh. It's easier to draft a long fiber than a short one. Especially for inexperienced spinners."

"So being a Wensleydale is a positive thing?"

"Yes. He's dependable, patient . . . I'm getting all mystical . . . forgive me."

I told her about my psychic aroma sniffing. Lucy said uneasily, "Do I have a spiritual scent?"

The truth? No, I wouldn't tell her that the moment she slid into the Bronco I'd thought of bruised apples — the sour-sweet smell of damaged fruit. "Cream. Sweet cream."

"Thank you," she said in a low voice.

I had a bad feeling she knew I was dodging her. "So my brother's a tough, long, patient type of wool," I said as lightly as I could. "And Eve's a banana-scented —"

"Merino. She's merino. Soft, fine, but sturdy."

"I have a bad feeling I'm none of the above."

"You're a blend. Wensleydale, like Gus, but mixed with silk. Tussah silk."

"Isn't all silk made by worms? You're saying I'm tough and wormy?" I smiled.

"No. Strong and smooth. With the sheen of lovely daydreams."

I put an arm around her, slowly, gauging any sign of discomfort. When she didn't pull away, I gave her a gentle, sisterly hug. "What kind of wool are *you,* by the way?"

She kept looking at Gus's picture. "Angora rabbit."

"Hey, that's nice! Luxurious, fluffy . . ."

"Helpless and an easy catch for predators."

She clicked the phone off.

Tal Thinks of Bananas and Purple Sprinkles

You know it's special when the man you met twenty-four hours ago gets knocked in the head, and this thought runs through *your* head. *What would I do without him?*

I was quiet, distracted, as I drove Doug, Eve, and Teasel back to Free Wheeler that evening. Darkness, gray and peppered with cold drizzle, closed around us. Lucy's gift for Gus made a warm weight on my lap: a handsome scarf in a rich steel-gray yarn — Wensleydale, of course. I'd talked her into posing with it as I snapped a photo using Doug's phone. Her face looked ethereal and luminous, framed by her pale, white-blond hair. Her large eyes were pensive. She gazed straight into the lens while cradling the scarf to her shoulder as if it were a baby.

I texted the photo to Gus with this message:

MEET MY PAL LUCY. FIBER ARTIST. I'M SENDING YOU THIS SCARF SHE MADE.

Bumpity bump. The tires of Doug's big veterinary rig rumbled as we entered the old lane to Free Wheeler. "Take it easy now," Doug called jovially. "I've lost a few brain cells already, today." He sat by the passenger window with his right elbow propped on its sill and that hand holding Lucy's towel-wrapped ice pack to his head. Teasel stood on the floorboard between his knees, chewing a candy wrapper. Eve, seated between Doug and me, chattered happily to him now that she understood he wasn't badly hurt. Although she *was* disappointed that he wouldn't be turning into a unicorn.

I slowed down. His truck was like driving a small tank; instead of a bed, it had a customized compartment outfitted with a fridge for medicines, a sterilized water tank, specialized implements, and even an ultrasound unit.

Eve launched into a description of the "Be A Safety Bee" talk she'd gone to while Lucy and I went to the bunker. There were several children Eve's age at the farm, and Macy regularly gathered them into one of the small classrooms for chats and homeschooling.

". . . and so Macy says that that's what to do if someone scary comes to see your mommy."

". . . that's exactly right, sweetheart," Doug was telling her. "You call . . ."

A herd of deer leapt across the lane in front of us, and I concentrated on slowing down without stomping the brake.

It didn't help my nervous mood that, as we were climbing into the truck, Macy had furtively tucked a special present into the pocket of my hoodie. "Condoms," she whispered, winking. "In case you need to keep any purple sprinkles out of your fondant."

It was going to be an interesting night.

CHAPTER FIVE

Doug Enjoys the Attention

Nine o'clock on that rainy November night, and all was going my way. I had my oldest soft gray sweats on, the ones that I've owned since the boxing team at university — okay, I admit it, a full seventeen years ago. I've washed them so much that they've gone thin and clingy around my best parts. A legacy!

My eyes were pretending to be asleep. The fat wooden lamp on my night table was putting out a warm glow of light, and I was cozy-hard under a king-sized plaid quilt (Firth clan colors) that the Rainbow gang had stitched for me the spring before in barter for delivering five calves and treating an abscess on Ripley, Alberta's chow-poodle rescue. Ripley is named after Sigourney Weaver's kick-ass character in the *Alien* movies.

Ripley bit me.

Tal eased into my bedroom every two hours to make sure I wasn't dead. To be precise, she woke me up long enough to count her upheld fingers and prove she wasn't blurry. Sure, it could be that I'd suffered a mild concussion, yes.

Around seven p.m. I'd mumbled about getting up to feed Zanadu and Pammy their evening oats, but she'd already done that. She'd also fed Teasel, the pigs, plus all the dogs and kitties.

What a woman.

Honestly, I felt good except for the sore knot at the edge of my rusty-red hairline. It was about an inch wide but had gone down from an equal inch tall to oh, just a half-inch tall. The color was ripening into a deep pink filigreed with darker pink splotches. Teasel hopped up on my bed from time to time and licked it. Maybe he thought I was growing an apple.

Once again, I heard Tal's footsteps on the hall floor then muffled on the braided rug beside my bed. I inhaled her feminine scent, her cooking aroma, too. Something lemony. Sweet. Cookies? A pie? My stomach growled. The aura of her body's warmth merged with mine. A cool, soft pressure caressed my cheek: the backs of her fingers, testing my okay-ness.

I shifted and made a low sound of pleasure in my throat, just enough to indicate I was sleepy and comfortable but not come across as hard as a rock and wanting so badly to hold her. She stroked my cheek, brushed the hair back from my forehead without hurting the knot, smoothed my quilt and sheets over my chest, then bent closer. Her lips brushed my hair; I heard the delicate *smuff* of her kiss as they met and pulled apart.

I opened my eyes. I think she knew I had been awake the whole time. We traded a look that said it all. I gave the slightest jerk of my head. *Come on, come here.* Wince. Maybe she'd feel sorry for me?

"Oh, Doug," she whispered, "what are we going to do?"

"I have plenty o' suggestions for tonight."

"Tonight's choices are simple. I can't resist. But the rest is hard."

Aye, it's very hard, but not in the way you think. The rest is easy.

I pulled an arm free of the covers and clasped her hand as it lay gently on my chest. She wound her fingers through mine. A good sign. "If you'll be my guest here in this bed after Eve is sound asleep, I swear that your mind can rest at ease. I'm not himself, that bastard up in New York. I

166

won't trick you, use you, or desert you — or Eve. To be blunt about it, I'm armed with protection, and I know how to use it."

She smiled and looked a bit awkward but told me Macy had given her some defenses as well.

"Good, then. We've an understanding. And if those efforts fail, I'll not run from the responsibility. I think I'd make a good *dah,* although you might find me letting the wee ones run wild with the goats and such." She began chuckling. *"And,* just so you know, I've taken a shine to Eve, and I believe that's mutual. I'd be proud for her to think of me as her *dah."*

She looked down at me tenderly. "Are you sure you don't have a concussion?"

"I see one — and only one — woman before my eyes."

She gently kissed the bump on my forehead. Something about the mix of pain nerves and pleasure nerves nearly lifted me off the mattress. Before I could finish my gasp she put her mouth to mine. I curled my arm around her as we sank together, trading the kind of deep, wet, hot kiss that put us inside each other's bodies.

When we broke apart, breathing hard, she said hoarsely, "We have to think this through . . . we have to . . ."

I pulled her down to me, and we kissed another long time, barely moving except for our heads, her sitting beside me on the bed but not laying next to me. All very demure except for the act of joining with kisses and the promise of joining in other ways.

She tore away from me, smooched me hard on the nose, and ordered, "Get up *now*, for dinner. Eve's in your office coloring on a note pad with your crayons." She laughed weakly, looking down at me with tearful and lustful eyes. "I need to know why you own a giant pack of crayons. I need to know a *lot* more about you. Please."

I sat up, catching her around the shoulders with the crook of my arm, her not pulling away, and I said, "They're treats. For Teasel. He eats them like candy."

She burst out laughing again, took my face between her hands, and kissed me a dozen times while holding me at bay. She let me go, but then I pulled her back. By the next time we escaped from each other, we were panting.

"Dinner," she said, pleading. I let her go, and she scrambled off the bed and left the room.

Tal Enjoys Foreplay with Scrapbooks

Unaware that Doug and I were trading an entire *Kama Sutra* full of coded glances over plates of my made-from-scratch chicken pot pie, Eve merrily crayoned sheep, cupcakes, and naked stone ladies onto a notepad while watching *Finding Nemo* for the fiftieth time, thanks to Doug's Netflix subscription. Every pet on the place was sprawled or curled or draped around her. Cats, dogs, pigs.

Teasel nuzzled her for crayons. Doug told him, *No more.* Teasel had reached his limit for the day.

Doug's office-den was a wonderfully cozy world of soft leather couches, an old desk with a brass giraffe-head lamp, shelves stuffed with books, and woodsy keepsakes. I tried to believe that the raccoon skull next to the bird's nest was not staring at us. A fire crackled on a stone hearth near our feet, which were propped on a coffee table he'd built from weathered shipping pallets and decorated with rusty hinges.

He'd changed the top of his gray sweat-suit for a long flannel shirt. Good idea, since the thin material of the bottoms needed a privacy curtain. My pink-socked feet looked so *right* next his nubbly gray socks. The couch was like sinking into a leather marshmallow. The cushions sloped toward the couch's middle, inspiring us to slide closer to each other, caught in a supercharged lull between discovery and fulfillment. Serene anticipation. I worried about the future, not about tonight.

"Come closer," he said coyly, setting his empty plate down and crooking a finger at me. With his other hand he reached for a thick three-ring binder he'd placed on the coffee table. "I want to show you my scrap-book collection."

I set my plate down too, then eased across the last six inches separating us. When my denimed thigh met his thinly cottoned one, we both exhaled silent *ah's*. "I'm a very sheltered lady," I protested in a fey tone. "So I do hope you're not planning to show me anything shocking."

He opened the binder with a flourish. "Naked bicycles."

Free Wheeler came to life in all its sketched and photographed glory.

My face grew warm and the rest of me even warmer. I busied myself turning scrap-book pages. "I'd love to have seen it first-hand. To have been there."

"Ah, me, too."

"What I said to Jay Wakefield about his personality?"

"Smelling like a mushroom. I loved it."

"There's a good person hiding inside him. Maybe he'll reconsider his plan."

"We'll enlist Delta to talk to him. She claims he's another of her cousins. Like you, like me, like everyone on the planet."

"So . . . you and I are cousins?"

"Not of the seriously genetical kind."

"Genetical?"

"Lovely word. I made it up."

"You don't let the rules of English stand in your way when a made-up word is better?"

"I'm Scots. Barely speak English as it is, and proud of that fact."

"Do you speak Scottish?"

"By that you mean Gaelic. Yes, I do. A bit."

"Say something to me."

He thought for a moment, touched my hand, and said quietly, *"Tha gaol agam ort."*

I managed a rough sound-alike. *"Hah GEUL AH-kum orsht.* What does it mean?"

"It's a secret. I'll tell you later."

"Ah hah."

A soft snore came from in front of the television. Teasel was stretched out on his side, little hooves twitching in a goatly dream. Snoring. Eve was sound asleep also, her notepad and crayons in her lap. She used Teasel's shoulder as a pillow. The pit

171

bulls were curled on either side of her, and Leo, the orange Maine coon, was draped over both them and Eve.

I covered my mouth to keep from laughing too loudly, and Doug said to the rest of the menagerie — dogs, cats, the two small pigs — "Can you not get up and dance about, you slackards? Play yon piano, or look grumpy, or ride a Roomba? Do you not understand that we're on the verge of YouTube *gold,* here?"

Suddenly, I realized I was happy. Serene in a way I barely recognized. My childhood had been filled with sadness and insecurity, even after the Rodriquez's became our foster family. Gus, Gabby, and I were close-knit but had very different personalities, and as soon as Gus turned eighteen, he left us — deserted us, is how Gabby puts it when she's in a mood — for the army. He wanted to honor Daddy's service in the military and police, but also, there was trouble between him and our foster parents. Their seventeen-year-old daughter, Miranda, announced that she intended to marry him and/or have his baby. Was he guilty of encouraging her to love him? Did he have feelings for her? Had he resisted the urge to sample the intimate cupcake she offered him? Yes, yes but no.

His family bond with the Rodriquez's

snapped the moment they learned that their Catholic school honor student had been deflowered by him. They felt betrayed, and he admitted they were right to feel that way. Gus makes mistakes, but he takes full responsibility, sometimes too much so. He was banished from their home, but Gabby and I were still underage and remained behind, treated with affection and respect. Gus joined the army, putting a permanent kink in Gabby's relationship with him, and left me feeling lonelier than ever. I wandered through high school, bounced out of college, headed to New York for culinary school, went to work for Mark, got pregnant, raised Eve (I can't imagine my life without her, and I feel blessed to have her), and struggled to keep us afloat via my tiny bakery. Never feeling settled, never feeling comfortable. Never having a plan except to keep working and hope that someday I'd figure out who and what and why I was.

Now I had landed where I belonged.

Home. Hearth. Doug.

At least, for tonight.

The Man of the Family

I carried Eve to the guest bedroom, watched Tal tuck her and Teasel under the covers, then fetched a baby monitor I kept in my truck for nights when I dozed in barns next to a seriously ill patient. "As long as we hear Teasel snoring," I told Tal, "we'll know Eve's still fast asleep."

"Mommy?" Eve said, squinting up at us and yawning, thus putting the lie to *still fast asleep*.

Tal bent over her, stroking her red hair. "Yes, sweetie?" The sight of them together, in my house, depending on me and comfortable with my presence made me feel more like a man than I'd ever felt before in my life.

"Are you going to stay awake and make sure Doug doesn't die?"

Tal went "*Uht,*" in surprise, and then, "Well . . ."

I put in, "Would you mind if she did, Eve? If she visited with me awhile? Would that be all right with you?"

Eve nodded and yawned again. "Sure. That's what grown-ups do."

Tal softly explained about the monitor I'd put on the nightstand. "If you need anything, just yell 'Mommy,' and I'll come running."

"Hmmm." Eve draped an arm over Teasel. "Love you."

Tal kissed her forehead. "Love you too, sweetie."

Eve opened one eye and looked up at me. "Love you, Doug. You don't have to say it back. You're a boy."

My throat closed and some sort of dust got into my eyes. If I promised her something Tal wasn't ready for me to promise, I'd be sorry. But how could I not say it back? Tal shook her head at me but didn't seem upset. In fact, she looked awkwardly concerned. Not good for a woman's love life when her child starts verbally stalking a new boyfriend.

I gave her a reassuring look. And then to Eve, I said, "If I say it back, will I turn into a girl?"

She giggled. "I don't think so."

"Then I love you, too."

She smiled. "I knew it." The smile faded. Her breath slowed. She slept.

Teasel snored.

I held out my hand to Tal. Her eyes gleamed. I'd said the right thing. And I'd meant it.

She took my hand, and I led her out of the room, gently closing the door behind us.

A Time for Passion

"What's your favorite color?" he whispered. He was on top of me, inside me, his face softly lit in the glow of a small bedside lamp. We were both dewy and limp — well, not completely limp, *ever.*

"Pale blue," I whispered. I stroked my bare toes down the backs of his legs, giving special TLC to the scars. He had several nasty ones from being dragged, kicked, or bitten in his work. I'd kissed them all.

"Favorite sport?"

"This one. You've turned me into an avid fan."

He smiled. "Favorite sport second to this one, though 'tis hard to think of anything remotely as fun."

"Your brogue gets deeper at times, you know?"

"Aye, when I'm excited. You've near got me speakin' in tongues." He shifted inside me, and I squeezed him with my thighs. "Stop it, ya wild lass! I'll na be kin to spake ta me clients aboot their wee beasties!"

I laughed. He groaned and nudged me so deeply I gasped. "Your fav'rite sport, woman! Talk!"

"Baseball."

"Good! I was afraid you'd say soccer or golf."

"Why?"

"Because everyone thinks that's all a Scotsman cares about."

"You don't like soccer or golf?"

"I like them fine, but American baseball has won my heart."

"What team?"

"National? The Cardinals. Local? The Asheville Tourists."

"Asheville has a pro baseball team now?" I ran my fingers over his shoulders and neck then up into his damp, russet hair.

"Farm team of the Colorado *Rockies.*"

"That's amazing. The city has grown a lot since we left."

He stroked my wildly messed-up hair and studied me tenderly. "Tell me about that time. When you were a child."

"Right now? No. It's . . . it's too sad. I don't want to change the mood."

He smiled gently. "You underestimate my ability to ignore every emotion except the one you feel twitching down yon." His smile segued into something quieter, more serious. "Tell me one little bit, then. Don't think about it. Say the one thing that comes to your mind the easiest. That's usually what's most important. All right? When I say 'Tell,' you say it?"

I nodded, already feeling tears sting my eyes.

He cupped my face between his hands,

kissed me on the nose, then said gruffly, *"Tell."*

"After Mama died, we were sent to foster parents who ran a farm outside Asheville. Delta tried to get custody of us, but there were screw-ups in the paperwork. An elderly neighbor tried to take us in, but he was an alcoholic with a criminal history, so that went nowhere. We were in limbo and ended up with strangers. The man was mean to us; he just wanted free labor. When Gus backtalked him, he locked Gabby and me in an unlit, cold shed. Told Gus we could stay there until we starved unless Gus apologized. Gus hit him with a tractor wrench. Hurt him, probably badly. I remember seeing a lot of blood before Gabby covered my eyes.

"Gus loaded us into the man's truck and drove us back to Asheville. We went to our elderly neighbor — I wish I could remember his name. He took us to the bus station and bought us tickets for California. He knew some people there, the Rodriquez's. He never told anyone where he'd sent us. Not even Delta." I took a deep breath. "None of us came back to North Carolina again, until now. It's the reason we've sidestepped all of Delta's invitations. Bad memories."

Doug had gone completely still, body and

spirit; his gaze was focused intensely on my face. He stroked a thumb over my brow then over the tears seeping from the corners of my eyes. "How old were you?" he asked gruffly.

"About six, I think. Gabby was eight. Gus was twelve." I blinked rapidly, trying to fan the tears away. "This is why I didn't want to talk about it. I knew it would ruin this lovely night. One of the best nights of my life."

"Mine, too. Ssssh. And nothing's ruined. In fact, it's even better, now."

"Why?"

"Because now I understand why you look so sad to me sometimes and why you have such a kindness of manner about you. You bring out something in people that's special. Something in me that makes me better than I was." He bent his head beside mine, lowering the full weight of his chest onto my breasts. He whispered to me in Gaelic, his tone hungry, his emphasis very specific. I didn't need a translator to understand the message. When he drew back to study my reaction, he obviously liked what he saw. "You've gone all pink," he said. He moved inside me, hardening. "And you feel wonderfully pink elsewhere, too."

I drew him down to me.

Tal Considers the Future

I was lucky to have had a father who loved my mother and vice versa. Lucky to have a sister and brother who would always be there for me. Lucky to have a daughter I liked as well as loved and who liked/loved me in return.

Lucky to have finally found a man I admired, respected, liked, and could not imagine leaving.

But what if I had to?

Brooding about the unknown future, I roamed Doug's house the next morning, pretending it was my home, too. I straightened and dusted. I polished and swept. Then I baked until there was no flour left, a few ounces of milk, and only one egg. Wheat bread, an apple pie, oatmeal cookies, pumpkin bread, yeast rolls and, of course, biscuits. It dawned on me that I was filling his pantry with memories of me. A substitute.

Doug had gone out the door at six a.m., whistling and kissing me goodbye. He'd be back at mid-morning to drive Eve and I to the café for the day. Our wonderful night had transitioned smoothly into a comfortable family morning. I never wanted it to end.

Armed with a stethoscope Doug had given her, Eve was checking heartbeats on the pigs. Then she prodded their snouts and solemnly told them, "I need to look at your throats. Say 'Oink.'" I watched her feed Teasel a crayon snack, and that's when it hit me. She was happier than I'd ever seen her before. What would it do to her to go back to New York? What if Mark fought for shared custody and won?

I sat down at the kitchen table with a second scrapbook Doug had given me. I browsed more articles about Clapper bicycles and looked at old photos Doug had collected with the help of Pike Whittlespoon's elderly uncle. I saw the years go by quickly; the sepia give way to Kodachrome, the clothing changed from victorian to modern. Beards vanished, women's hair grew shorter, their skirts grew shorter and slimmer, too; they wore cloche hats and showed their ankles.

But always at the center of it all, with his trademark handlebar mustache, was Arlo Claptraddle. And nearby, if not right next to him, was the redhead, no doubt the one who'd inspired that rose-waving image on the mosaic. I was betting the Spinning Rose bicycle was named after her. I searched for her name but couldn't find one. I did, however, find the name, and photo, of Arlo's wife.

The former Dorothy Seymour of Savannah, Georgia attends the Governor's Ball in Raleigh, 1926. Known to her friends as "Dot," Mrs. Osserman is active in fundraising and can often be found hosting parties in Savannah's historic Seymour mansion, as well as at the Osserman estate in Raleigh. Her husband, Samuel Arlo Osserman, is a noted inventor and manufacturer.

Samuel Arlo Ossserman? Arlo Claptraddle's real name?

Dot Osserman was small, pretty, elegant, and dark-haired. As I read more articles about her society schedules, one thing became clear in a hurry: Dot spent a lot of her time somewhere besides these mountains.

I went to Doug's office and retrieved the first scrapbook then spread both it and the other one open on the table. I began skimming, looking for clues to the mystery. Where did Rose fit in? Each time I spotted her in a photograph, I noted the year. She hadn't appeared in these chronicles of Free Wheeler until the late nineteen thirties.

A year or two before she was immortalized in the mosaic.

I turned a page, and there she was ten years later, in a yellowed color snapshot from 1947, not as part of a crowd, but this time . . . just her and Arlo, surrounded by fat dogs and cats . . . sitting together on the . . . *the front steps of this house.* Someone had scrawled ROSE DOOLEY, ARLO'S COOK AND HOUSEKEEPER across her legs.

Ping. Something was familiar. Not just the house, but in their faces. He was much older than she, starting to go gray. Something sad had begun to lurk in his eyes. The younger Arlo had looked exuberant, always smiling. This Arlo looked worried. No surprise. The Depression and World War Two hadn't been good for the bicycle business. In fact, during the war he'd shut down. Materials were scarce. Metal, rubber — all went to the factories building tanks, airplanes, guns. People even sold their kitchen grease. The glycerin in it was needed for bombs.

Rose Dooley looked . . . young. Comfortable. Down to Earth. She wore dungarees, a plaid shirt, and an apron. Her elbows rested on her aproned knees, and her hands floated in the air between them. Her hair was plaited over one shoulder. She leaned just a little toward him, and he toward her. They sat at least a foot apart, but body language, as I'd proved to Doug more than once last night, speaks louder than words.

Exactly what did she do with *her* glycerin?

An absentee wife from high society. A young mountain girl who came to work for a fascinating older man — a quirky inventor with a big, lonely house — and bed — to fill. Hmmm.

"Whatcha lookin' at, Mommy? You're puckered."

Puckered was our word for frowning.

I sat back, relaxing my squint of gossipy concentration. "There. Now I'm un-puckered." I started to suggest we explore The Hub again. She sat cross-legged on the kitchen floor with the pigs, Teasel, Leo, Fanny, Peaches and Bebe all sprawled around her. Her red hair trailed over one shoulder in a braid. She toyed with the stethoscope. Her hands finally settled on the knees of her jeans, lighting there briefly, like restless butterflies.

Ping.

"You're puckering up again," she said.

"Do me a favor? Go get one of your books, and let's do Reading Time."

"Yay!" She was up and out the kitchen door in a flash, trailed by her menagerie.

I pulled Doug's cell phone from my jeans' pocket, held the phone over the photo of Rose Dooley and Arlo, and snapped a picture. Then I texted it to Gabby in L.A. with the message:

WILL EXPLAIN LATER. DOES SHE LOOK FAMILIAR? P.S. WE'RE OKAY. I'M IN LOVE. TALK SOON.

Suddenly I realized it was only seven a.m. there.

I face-palmed. Gabby worked very late nights. Once again, I'd demonstrated the unending flakiness of Baby Sisterhood.

No. Not just no, this time, but Hell, No. I saw myself through Doug's eyes, now. Biscuit Witch, Cupcake Therapist, Mother Who Fights Off Pre-Diabetic Bears. A grown woman who had given herself whole-heartedly to a wonderful man. A man who had given himself to *me*.

I *earned* Doug. I *deserved* Doug.

I started to text Gabby again, a pre-emptive strike, something on the order of:

I KNOW IT'S EARLY THERE BUT THIS IS IMPORTANT.

My phone buzzed. I stared at the text from Gabby:

WHERE DID U GET PIX OF GRANDMA WITH SAM OSSER-MAN?

The dogs began to bark. "Mommy!" Eve

bounded past the doorway to the front hall. Her entourage galloped after her. "Some-body's coming! Maybe Doug's home early!"

"Go outside on the porch and see if it's him. Come back and tell me."

"Okay!"

I texted back:

GRANDMA? REALLY?

She answered:

THAT'S HER — FRM PIX MAMA HAD. I'VE GOT IT. BUT NOT SAM. JUST HER.

I texted:

YOU KNEW SAM O?

She replied:

OLD SAM WS OUR NEIGHBOR IN WEST ASHVL. HE PAID OUR WAY TO CALIFORNIA.

Typing feverishly, I texted:

SAM WAS THE ONE WHO HELPED US RUN AWAY? YES. VERY OLD.

FRAIL. BIG MUSTACHE. RODE BI-CYCLES.

I sat there, open-mouthed, stunned.

WE HV 2 TALK. I CALL YOU RIGHT NOW:

She answered:

CAN'T. I HAD BAD NITE, JMM CRASHED MY CATERING JOB. DON'T BELIEVE WHT U HEAR ON INTERNET GOSSIP THIS A.M. YES I DID STAB HIM WITH PICKLE FORK OK? IT WAS ACCIDENT. SOMEONE GOT ME OUT ON BAIL. MYSTERY FRIEND. MORE NEWS SOON.

"Mommy!" Eve rushed back, her face pale. "It's not Doug. It's a lot of men in a car. They look mean."

Showdown at Free Wheeler

"Doc, you're not always the most cheerful hoss in the barn, you know? So what I want to know is this." Burly Evers runs a herd of Jersey milk cows; he and his wife sell cow cheese to gourmet restaurants in Asheville. He pulled the pipe out of his beard hole and pointed the stem at me. "Are you on anti-depressors?"

I grinned as I finished loading my gear and shut the truck's compartment. "I've found the woman I want to marry."

Burly turned and bellowed at the pre-fab metal building where his wife, Gilda, and their daughters, Burl-Ann and Gilda Louise, were curdling a new tub of raw moo. Since the day was sunny and sixty degrees, they had a screened window open. "Gilda baby! Bring the doc a gift for his future wife-to-be!"

A good deal of whooping came from inside the building followed by a rush of large, round-faced female-hood dressed in white jumpsuits, rubber galoshes, and hairnets. After much hugging and back-patting, they handed me one of the kudzu-vine baskets they used for their gift sets at Turtleville's only wine shop, coffee bar, and "mountain tapas" café. In the basket were prettily wrapped blocks of cheese mixed with various herbs. Rosemary Cheese and Mint Cheese and Wild Dandelion Cheese, which was my personal favorite even though it always made me want to mow the yard.

Gilda sent her daughters back inside then pulled another block from the pocket of her jumpsuit. "Special blend," she said, winking. "Save it for nighttime when you and your lady don't gotta drive nowhere."

Burly hooted. I thanked them but stored that one in the truck's refrigerator behind a box of worming meds. The first time I ate the Special Blend cheese I spent an evening combing Leo and trying to count all the hairs on his ears. Five hundred twenty-three on the left ear; four thirty-nine on the right.

I climbed in my truck, waved to the Evers and their cows, and headed down their dirt road to the Asheville Trace. I had one more stop to make then I could head home for a couple of hours. Later that afternoon, I had a worming gig at an angus beef cattle farm outside Turtleville. Tal and Eve wanted to go with me on that one. What a woman! What a girl!

My cell phone beeped. I thumbed the controls. When Eve's frightened voice came out of the dashboard speaker, I stomped on the brake. "Mommy told me to stay in your office with the door locked and not make a peep, but Aunt Alberta said that when scary men come to see your mommy it's okay to call an adult and tell them about it, and a whole bunch of scary men are in the yard with Mommy . . ."

Five seconds later I was roaring toward home while phoning everyone in the neigh-

borhood to see which of us could get to
Free Wheeler the fastest.

Tal Learns a Lesson in Accepting Help

Mark had sent an offer. And reinforcements.
The duo from the first night now had three
assistants, all of whom were large, muscled,
and unsmiling.

"I'm listening," I said as calmly as pos-
sible, while my stomach churned.

The five of us stood in the front yard by
their rental car. They'd wanted to come
inside but changed their minds after I
threatened to let the dogs out. "Inside this
house are two pit bulls who don't like
strangers in general and men in particular."
Plus a really passive-aggressive little goat.
"If you take one step toward the veranda,
I'll let them out."

I prayed they'd believe me. Peaches and
Bebe had been thoroughly detoxed by
Doug's gentle care and training. They'd
probably charge out here and stage a violent
hand-licking. I'd have better luck ordering
Teasel and the pigs to attack.

"We'll stay right here," the leader conceded.

I wrapped a thick wool sweater tighter
around myself and tucked a fold over the
handgun in its pocket. "Good idea."

"Mr. Mark is willing to drop the assault charge."

"That's nice to know. My testimony would have embarrassed him. How he cornered me at my shop, threatened to ruin my business, and lunged at me. I punched him in self-defense, and I happened to have a fondant baby rattle in my fingers at the time. He swallowed it without any help from me."

"Look, he's trying to be reasonable. He just wants you to say you rejected his efforts to be part of Eve's life. That he didn't even know about her until a year ago."

"That's not true."

"And now that he does know, he wants to do the right thing. Be a father. Show his fans that he's a loving man with a wonderful daughter."

"Use her like a new puppy, take her for walks in Central Park, pretend to dote on her."

I heard the rumble of big tires on old cobblestone. Doug's vet rig. My skin chilled. He'd told me the truth about the confrontation at the café. These men carried guns and weren't afraid to pull them out. They pivoted toward the sound. The lead man fingered a swollen spot on his jaw.

"I don't want trouble," I said quickly.

"Neither do we. If that's Doug Firth, you better tell him to back off."

"I will. But you'd better worry about me, first." I lifted my little handgun from the sweater, just so they could see it. I stuck it back in the pocket.

He cursed.

The truck roared into the yard. Doug looked furious, no surprise. I held up one hand in a *calm down, it's under control* gesture. He shoved the truck into a blocking position near their car. As he stepped down from the tall rig, he brought a shotgun with him.

"I should have known," the leader said.

"Back the feck away from her," Doug told him in a low voice. He didn't point the shotgun at the group, but held it in a position that would easily swivel toward them.

The men stepped closer to their car. Doug planted himself in front of me, facing them. "You're all right?" he asked over his shoulder. "And Eve?"

"Yes. They're here to make a deal."

"You want to listen to them?"

"No, but I have to."

"Aw right, then. Hello, boys. How's the jaw, Fidgety?"

"We don't want another fight. We've mellowed out."

The second in command added, "Yeah, we've eaten a lot of shitty chicken burgers for the past two days. We just want this over with."

"Is that why you brought extra back-up?"

"If that hillbilly with the Jesus gun shows up, we'll need help." Fidgety turned his attention to me. "All you have to do is say none of this was Mr. Mark's fault. Just a misunderstanding. Sign over shared custody of Eve. Bring her to photo shoots and family vacations. Just put in appearances then go on your merry way."

"Not going to happen."

"In return, he'll pay child support covering the past five years *and* the next twenty. He'll take care of Eve — and you — in generous style, until she's twenty-five years old. He'll even prop up your cupcake business with a prime Manhattan location and plenty of marketing support."

"No. We're not going back to New York, and I'll never share custody of Eve. Isn't it enough that I'll *never* tell anyone he's Eve's biological father? He's not going to be part of her life, and he's not going to use her as a marketing prop."

"You're forcing him to play rough."

Doug said in a steely voice, "If you're making a threat, that's a big mistake."

"No, pal, you're the one making the mistake. Let me tell you how things really are. Delta Whittlespoon has a lot to lose in this situation." He paused. "And so do you."

I pushed forward. "What's that supposed to mean?" Doug pulled me behind him again.

Fidgety shrugged. "Mr. Mark owns fifty percent of *Skillet Stars.* I'm just saying."

"So if I don't cave in, he'll make sure Delta loses the final round?"

"I never said that, did I?"

"My cousin would rather lose that competition than hurt members of her family."

"Well, then, how about the consequences for him?" He jerked his head toward Doug. "He could get deported."

Doug quickly put in, "That's not going to happen, Tal. Don't worry about it."

"Oh, I'd worry about if I were you," Fidgety said. "Work visas have to be renewed regularly. His is up for consideration in a few months. What if somebody points out that he was involved in a fight and a shooting the other night? That he hid a woman who has a warrant out for her arrest? Maybe there'd even be allegations that he kidnapped Mr. Mark's daughter."

"That lie won't stand," Doug said. He

cocked the shotgun. "This conversation's over."

I took him by one arm. "We need to talk. In private. What he's saying is a possibility, isn't it?"

"I'll take my chances."

"I came here with a lot of baggage. I won't let it ruin everything you've worked for. Or Delta's dreams."

"Carrying your baggage? No problem. I'll even help you unpack it. Delta will say the same."

"There's no way to keep Eve from being told who her father is. If I took Mark's offer, at least I'd have money to enroll her in private schools and a great college. She'd have opportunities. Maybe she wouldn't have to pose as Mark's happy daughter for very long. Once the media attention died down . . ."

"Are you telling me you don't want to stay here? Is that it?"

"I don't really have any choice."

"You didn't answer my question."

"Yes, she did," Fidgety said. "Why don't you spare her the big break-up scene?" He pointed at me. "Go get your things. In two hours, you and the kid will be on a plane out of Asheville. End of adventure. All neat and done."

I ignored him and continued looking up at Doug, whose eyes showed the same pain I felt.

"I don't want you to get hurt. Let me go. I'm being torn apart."

"Tell me you don't love me," he ordered.

"This isn't about whether or not I . . ."

"Yes, it is about that that. Love's not just a word. It's a promise. A bond. I need to know."

"Doug, don't . . ."

"You realize the assault charge hasn't been dropped, yet," Fidgety announced. He jabbed a finger at me. "We can do this the hard way, where I come back with a deputy and he arrests mama bear here, and the state takes charge of the kid, and . . ."

I lunged at him. He'd said the magic words; had opened the door to a cage where I'd locked childhood memories of rage and despair.

I grabbed Fidgety's finger and wrenched it so hard I heard the joint pop. I tried to kick him in the groin next, but the other men grabbed me. I heard Doug make a sound of fury. The group tried to hold onto me and dodge his fists. I kicked one man in the knee and tripped on another's foot, going down hard. I slammed to the ground. Blood gushed from my nose.

"Run!" he yelled, trying to drag me to my feet. The quick thuds of several fists hitting him made him stagger.

They'll kill him.

I clambered to a stand and kicked Shark Eyes in the leg.

That's when the cavalry arrived.

Into the yard rumbled several big pick-up trucks from Rainbow Goddess Farm, followed by Cleo and Bubba in a minivan with a magnetized CROSSROADS CAFÉ sign on the driver's door. Fidgety was in pain and crouched over, cupping his injured hand with the other one, but his second in command, aka Shark Eyes, grabbed me by one arm and twisted it behind me while at the same time shoving me tight against the car. I was wedged between him and it. I elbowed him in the stomach. Doug was on the ground with three men on top of him, everyone slugging.

"Tell these crazy hillbillies to back off!" Shark Eyes yelled.

From the corner of one eye I saw Lucy hop out of a truck and run up the front steps. She tugged the front door open and went inside.

A gunshot split the air.

"I'm counting to fifteen and then *this* crazy hillbilly is going nuts!" Bubba bellowed. He waved his pistol at the treetops.

Two dozen women, including Macy and Alberta climbed out of the Rainbow Goddess trucks carrying enough fire power to take over a small country. Shake Eyes continued to clutch my twisted arm from behind. "We're just helping her. She fainted and hit her nose! She agreed to come with us. Her and her kid. Don't shoot!"

"Too late," Alberta said, lifting an M-16 to her shoulder and taking aim.

Beside her, Cleo hoisted a deer rifle. She sighted down the barrel at Fidgety, who was still bent over his hand. "Say hello to Satan," she said.

"Don't fire!" I yelled. "*Please.* Eve's inside, and this is terrifying enough for her without a shoot-out!"

"Mommy!" The door opened, and Eve darted out. Lucy was right behind her and made a grab, catching her around the waist. Lucy picked her up and ran past us down the steps, with Eve reaching back over Lucy's shoulders and screaming.

Teasel stepped out of the open doorway. He chewed his cud. He waggled his head like a cage fighter loosening up for a match. He charged.

Release the Kraken!

Teasel rammed sharp nubbins into the

back of Shark Eyes' knees. We went down in a heap. Doug shoved his way to us and punched Shark Eyes so hard his head snapped back.

"Doug, don't!" I yelled as Doug drew back a fist to smash him again.

"I'll kill the fecker!"

"Daddy, *stop*!"

Eve's plea cut through the chaos.

Eve strained toward us with only Lucy's grip on the tail of her shirt to keep her out of the fray. Lucy was sprawled on the ground "trying not to faint while lying down," she explained later. Still, she managed to keep Eve from squirming away. Eve's cheeks were streaked with tears as she looked from Doug to me and back to him. "Daddy," she repeated hoarsely. "I don't want you to get beat up anymore. You'll get another unicorn horn."

Fidgety stared at us. "Are you tellin' us the kid's not Mr. Mark's daughter?"

Silence. I looked up at Doug, who was breathing heavily and slowly unballing his fists. He had a bloody lip, one eye was swelling shut, and his knuckles were raw. The other men looked even worse.

"Doug," I said gruffly. I held up a hand. He reached down and took it, helped me up, and supported me with an arm around my shoulders when I wobbled. "You asked me two questions. The answers are 'No, I don't ever want to leave here,' and 'Yes, I love you.' But I want what's best for you as well as for Eve and me."

He gently wiped his fingertips across the blood beneath my nose. "I love you, too. What's best for me is to keep my family right here where we all belong." He sought Eve's upturned, hopeful face. "It's true," he said loudly. "I'm her father. Any man who makes claims otherwise is in for a fight."

Teasel butted Fidgety in the fidget.

Tal Embraces the Cove's Rowdy Attitude

The Crossroads Café is closed only four days a year: Christmas, Thanksgiving, Easter, and Family Reunion Saturday in mid-August when three hundred Whittlespoons and related families hold a gigantic lakeside barbecue at a campsite on the Hula Mae Reservoir just north of Turtleville. Or, as Bubba described it, "Hold My Beer And Watch This Day." Minor injuries are expected, with "minor" meaning anything that doesn't result in a spurting artery, amputation, permanent scar, or the loss of an internal organ.

The next day, it's back to work.

Since the brawl at Doug's house occurred

on an ordinary Thursday, we dabbed our wounds, escorted Fidgety and his crew to the county line, updated Gabby, told her Eve and I were moving to the Cove permanently, introduced her to Doug, relayed Jay Wakefield's offer (she went deadly quiet and got off the phone quickly, muttering something about payback), and then we drove to the café in time for me to bake the lunch biscuits.

Eve was pale and quiet, sitting on the steps of the kitchen porch with Lucy's gold-and-blue scarf wrapped around her and Teasel curled up by her side. Macy conducted an informal therapy session, with Doug and me watching worriedly. Slowly the color returned to Eve's face, and she began comfortably kicking the bottom steps, swinging her feet in an easy rhythm. She and Teasel shared some Gummy Bears.

I knew Mark would be thrilled to tell people the rumors about Eve had been proved completely false — that her "real" father had stepped forward. I baked Mark's name on a slip of paper in a soulless pan of unleavened bread and fed the bread to the crows out by the log-people nativity. A kind of hoodoo foodie curse.

Did it matter that Doug was not Eve's biological father? Nope. Didn't matter to

Doug, not to me, and not to Eve. We explained the truth to Eve in terms a precocious five-year-old could absorb.

"If a daddy decides not to be part of your life," I told her, "it's not a bad thing. In fact, it means there's a spot open for a daddy who really loves you."

As she listened to us describe how she came to be born and how much I loved her and how much Doug wanted to be her daddy, she twiddled her fingers in Teasel's wiry coat and finally said, "Okay, Mommy. Okay, Daddy. I'm a child of the universe. That's what Macy says. Can we go pick out a Christmas tree this afternoon?"

"Yes," we said in unison.

That was all she needed to hear. She grinned. Then she and Teasel went out in the yard to butt things with their heads.

Doug Gets Baked

Now I was a Man With A Reputation in the Cove. Meaning I had made my bones. I was a *made* Cove Man, who took care of his woman, his child, and his goat. A Southern mountaineer.

It's like joining the mafia, only with more guns.

"You know I'm a bad ass sumbitch now," I told Tal.

She kissed me. "I love your ass. It's not bad at all."

"That kind of talk will get you a good talking to."

My whole fecking body hurt, but I'd never been happier in my life. We were home, *home,* for the night; Eve sound asleep with Teasel and the rest of the animal pack, Tal curled up on the couch in front of the fire wearing naught but a soft set of long johns she'd gotten at the Cove store. The top was clingy, and the bottoms had a trap door that barely clung to its Velcro fasteners. I approved heartily. She held a glass of Scotch against her swollen nose and smiled at me over the rim. She liked how my sweatpants fit.

"A feast," I said, as I set a wooden tray filled with bread, cookies, and biscuits on the coffee table. "Many thanks to yourself. Did you try to bake up every bit of flour in the house this morning?"

She lowered the glass and studied its golden liquor for a moment, looking a bit sad. I settled beside her and pulled a quilt over our knees. "Were you trying to bake your worries away?" I asked gruffly. "To leave something for me to remember you by?"

She nodded, getting teary. I dabbed her

eyes. She took a deep breath. "Last night, when you spoke that Gaelic phrase to me. You said it was a secret. You'd tell me what it meant, later. Okay, so would you tell me, now?"

"Tha gaol agam ort," I repeated softly. *I love you.*

"Tha gaol agam ort," she whispered. "Did I say that right? I might have just vowed to do your taxes."

"No, you said it right. Say it again."

She did, her eyes gleaming. Then she kissed me gently on my bruised mouth. 'Twas highly unlikely either one of us would do more than snuggle, given our condition. On the other hand, with a little extra medication for our tense muscles . . .

I leaned over the tray of goodies, split a warm slice of pumpkin bread in two, decorated the pieces with a generous smear of cheese, then sat back and held one out to her. "Remember what I told you about the Evers family and their special cheese?"

Her eyes widened. She smiled.

We might only sit up 'til dawn counting each other's freckles, but that would be just fine.

Gabby Dodges; Lucy Is on the Radar

Our Christmas tree was spectacularly edible. Since Doug owned no ornaments, we covered it in strings of popcorn, candy canes, red bows, gingerbread men, and several strands of retro bubble lights, which were fascinating to watch after he and I shared the last of the special cheese. Teasel and the pigs ate everything off the lower branches except the lights. Eve and I redecorated the bare spots with pine cones dipped in glitter. Teasel ate a couple of those then gave up.

Doug and I talked for hours about Free Wheeler and Jay, trying to come up with an alternate plan that might win him over. I spent a lot of time on the phone with Gabby, trying to unravel the mystery of Sam Osserman and our grandmother. Was Sam our grandfather?

"You have to come here and see Free Wheeler," I told her. "Whether we have a legacy here by blood or just because Grandma Nettie spent so many years working here . . . it's a magical place. We could bring it back to life, not as a bicycle factory, but maybe as . . ."

"I'm not working for a Wakefield," she snapped. "Ever."

"Is there anything you want to tell me

about Jay?"

"No."

"Gabby, when you don't tell me the truth, I smell vinegar. Right now I could pickle an entire bushel of cucumbers with the scent."

"Let's just leave it at this, Baby Sister: you're too young to remember the name of Mama's landlord — the man who cancelled her lease when she missed just *one* payment on the diner's rent. His name was E.W. Wakefield."

My jaw dropped. "Oh, no."

"Oh, yes. Jay's greedy uncle. That was the last straw. She'd lost Daddy. Then she lost the diner. It killed her. *E.W. Wakefield killed her.*"

I clamped a hand to my forehead. "Why didn't you tell me this before?"

"I was hoping you'd drop the whole subject."

"Okay, okay, we're not doing business with a Wakefield, period. But we still have to tell Gus about the offer. Who's going to tell him? You or me?"

"Neither. He has enough on his plate. I'm worried about him. He seems burned out. As if trying to save the world through cooking diplomatic dinners on desert campfires is useless. Which it is. Useless."

"But it's not fair to keep this secret. I'm

done keeping secrets from my loved ones."

"He's said a hundred times that he's career military and not interested in anything else. What makes you think he'll suddenly come home — to North Carolina, a place where none of us have many happy memories . . ."

"That's not true. Before Mama and Daddy . . ."

"Look, you've found a great guy and a home you love there, so more power to you. But it's not for me, and it's not for Gus."

"I'll tell him about the offer from Jay, regardless. I wouldn't feel right not to. What Jay's uncle did . . . we can't blame Jay for that."

"Trust me, he's no better than his uncle. A liar."

"What? Why do you say . . ."

"Okay, okay. Save the talk with Gus until after Christmas, at least. You know this time of year is hard for him."

"All right. I agree. Look, could you *please* get on a plane and come here for the holidays? Just for a day or two. Meet Doug. Come and hang out."

"I'll think about it. I've got a lot going on. Meeting with my lawyers. Fighting the lawsuit and the bogus assault charge."

"Hey, that runs in the family. Did you ever

find out who the mystery man is? The one who paid your bail?"

"Gotta run, kiddo. I've got pickles in the boiler. Love you. Love to Eve. Love to Doug. I want to meet him soon. Et cetera. Buh bye."

Click.

The pungent aroma of vinegar grew stronger. Gabby was a pickler, a lover of spices, brines, pepper sauces, gourmet salts, fine vinegars and All Things Not Sweet. She distrusted the gentle lure of sugar and believed life is a taste test where Sour trumps Sweet every time. If she lost Vin E. Garr's, she'd have to go back to work as a sous chef for a Napa Valley hotel where hipsters complained that her seasonings irritate their nose rings.

I sat there brooding about her evasive attitude. My phone buzzed. Gus, texting me. It had been several days since I'd sent him the photo of Lucy holding the scarf she'd picked for him. That scarf, along with the huge box of food, was winging its way to Afghanistan.

Her photo popped up in his reply. I sucked in a breath as I read his cheerfully macho message:

SEND THE SCARF AND THE

BLONDE. I WANT HER NUMBER.

No way would I encourage him to contact Lucy. It would be like turning a well-intentioned bull loose in a very fragile china shop.

The Spinning Rose

The three of us had just finished a breakfast of pecan waffles and scrambled eggs. I had to admit it: Katie Dood's free-range, TV watching hens gave premium egg love.

Doug got up from the table and stretched. "I know Christmas is still a couple of weeks off, but . . . well, I've got something for Eve. It's not really a Christmas present. It's more of an early birthday gift. I'll be right back."

As he went outside, Eve whispered to me, "My birthday's not 'til July."

"Daddy likes to plan ahead."

I got up and held the kitchen door open.

Doug guided the Spinning Rose inside. He'd cleaned her dusty red paint, polished her, replaced the brittle leather handgrips with rubber ones, and added brand-new modern tires plus a set of training wheels. The rose-handled umbrella was in rehab, needing more work, but the wicker basket gleamed with a fresh coat of golden varnish.

Eve gasped. With her hands to her mouth

in awe, she tiptoed to her great-grandmother's namesake bicycle, perhaps even the very bicycle Emma Nettie had ridden herself. She touched the handlebars gently. "It has a heartbeat," she whispered.

Delta's on the Line

"Delta's on the phone from New York," Cleo said. "She wants to talk to you both." Cleo set an aging speaker phone between us on the café's gingham table cloth. It was mid-afternoon on a Monday, and the café was empty. In a few hours the tables would fill with a pre-Christmas Eve crowd of friends gathering to watch the newest installment of *Skillet Stars* on several large TV sets scattered around the dining rooms. Since that show was about to start taping in one hour, we were surprised that Delta called.

Cleo tapped the phone's faded black plastic. "This is the phone that Delta had Tom Mitternich use when Tom pretended to be Cathy's husband so he could coach her through her physical therapy in the burn ward in Los Angeles. This phone is *sacred.*" She paused. "The volume goes in and out. You'll have to hunker close, and you may have to shout for Delta to hear you."

Doug and I smiled at each other over cups

of tea. I was dusty with flour, dressed in jeans and a sweatshirt, an apron and running shoes. Doug wore sweat-stained overalls, because he'd just come from vaccinating a small herd of bison.

"I'm nervous," I said.

"Me too, a bit. It's like getting a call from the President."

The phone line crackled. "Hi y'all!" Delta shouted. "What's cooking?"

I put a hand over my heart. Suddenly, I had tears in my eyes. "I am. Cooking, that is. I just made five pans of biscuits in your kitchen. I'm humble in your shadow, Cousin."

"Oh, piss-shaw. We're both biscuit witches, honey, just like your mama and Mary Eve Nettie. And like your grandma, Emma."

I sucked in a breath. "Was Emma known as Rose Dooley?"

"Yes, baby, she changed her name when she left Asheville and went into hiding at Free Wheeler."

"Who was she hiding from?"

"Augustus Damn Wakefield, that's who. Rich old horndog. Wanted her biscuits for his private kitchen, if you know what I mean."

Doug and I traded a shocked look. It was bad enough about Jay's family connection to Mama losing the diner, but now this, too?

"Not that he needed a wife," Delta went on. "He had two of those already. One in Asheville, for show, and another one locked up in a sanatorium up in Virginia. People said the only reason that one went crazy was from being married off to Augustus."

"So my grandmother hid her identity to escape from him and went to work as a cook in Free Wheeler for Arlo Claptraddle — Sam Osserman?"

"Yep. Sam was Jewish, from a fine old family down in Georgia. He wasn't cut out for ordinary ideas. Kind of a dreamer. Married who they told him to marry, but there wasn't anything but politeness between him and his wife. When he got an inheritance, he disappeared into the mountains, reinvented himself with a funny name, and built his bicycle world. Your grandma came along, and it was love at first sight." She chuckled. "I'm guessing you and Doug believe in that, don't you?"

I nodded as Doug bent over the phone. "Tagger saw her first. I stole her from him."

Delta laughed.

I asked quietly, "What happened to Emma and Sam? All my brother and sister and I know is that our grandmother died after Mama was born. We never knew who our grandfather was. But the man Gabby and Gus called "Old Mr. Sam" was our neighbor. He tried to take care of us. Do you know who our grandfather was?"

"Honey, can't you see the jelly on the crust?"

"You're saying for certain that it was Sam — Arlo Claptraddle?"

"I sure am. Sam was your grandpa."

I sat there in silence, dazed.

We heard noises in the background. An instantly recognizable female voice said, "Time to wax your eyebrows, Cuz."

Delta said to Cathy Deen Mitternich, "Can't my eyebrows have a day off, for once?"

"Beauty is in the eye of the beholder. But beauty is also in the eyebrow of the *beholdee.*"

Cathy Deen Mitternich's voice. The actress. Delta's cousin. Thus, *my* cousin. In a world of six degrees of separation, I was *this* close to a Hollywood celebrity armed with hot wax and a pair of tweezers.

"Look, I've gotta go," Delta said to us. "I'll fill you in on the rest later. For now, just chew on this chunk of taffy: Augustus Wakefield ruined Sam out of jealousy and revenge because of Emma. He bought the bank that held a big loan Sam took out during the lean years of World War Two. When Sam missed a payment, Augustus foreclosed. Took Free Wheeler as the collateral."

Doug and I were stunned. He said slowly, "I always thought Arlo just fell on hard times. But he didn't fall. He was pushed."

"That's right, Doc. A Wakefield family tradition."

I caught my breath. "You mean . . . Jay's uncle cancelled Mama's lease because she was Emma's daughter? Because of an old feud that happened decades earlier between his father and Grandma Emma?"

"I don't doubt it."

"Why did he give Mama and Daddy that lease in the first place?"

"Control, baby. Wakefields are all about control. They get people under their thumbs and then pull the rugs out from under them when they're at their weakest point."

Doug said, "I just can't believe Jay's cut from that same cloth."

"I hope you're right. Hold onto your rugs, you two. There's more. Sam went berserk. Showed up at the Wakefield offices in Asheville and tried to kill Augustus. Sam served five years in prison."

I sagged. I felt Doug's gentle hand on mine and looked at him tearfully. "What happened to Emma?" I asked.

"She was pregnant with your mama when Sam went to prison. Mary Eve brought her to Wild Woman Ridge and tried to soothe her, but she was just heartbroken. She lost her mind a little bit. Mary Eve would find her at Free Wheeler, walking the empty streets, talking to people as if they were still there, talking to Sam as if he were right beside her, and sleeping in the boarded-up house. It was too hard for her. She died of an infection a few days after your mama was born."

Tears slid down my face. Doug wound his fingers through mine and tugged. I nodded at him. *I'm okay. You're here. I'm not alone the way she was. The way Mama was, too. I've got you.*

"Delta, why didn't you tell us that once we were grown?" I asked hoarsely.

"Because I figured the story would keep you away forever or else send you down a path of revenge. I kept looking for ways to lure the three of you home, first. Figured once I got even one of you locked safe in the bosom of the family, you could handle the rest."

I chuckled despite my tears. "So I'm the first catch?"

"Yep. You fell right into my plan. Doug, too."

He rubbed the sadness from his own eyes and said in a grand voice, "Have you got any plans for world peace? Solving the troubles in the Middle East? And perhaps some way to keep the Koreans from coming up with another *Gangnam Style?*"

"Sure. All it takes is sharing food and respect. It's that simple. What was that last one? The Koreans are ganging up on Gomer Pyle? Since when? Dear Lard, look at the time. Okay, okay, I'm going. Get that stuff away from me! I don't want any more mousse in my hair. Not even one tiny little mouse-dab of mousse."

To us: "Here's what y'all need to know in a nutshell. Tom's been helping me do a little investigating. Free Wheeler still belongs to Sam! And that means to his kin! His only heirs! And that means *you,* Tal. You and Gabby and Gus."

Open-mouthed, Doug and I looked from the phone to each other, then back at the phone. He leaned into its air space. "Jay Wakefield's a lot of things, but I don't believe he's a thief. If there's proof he doesn't own the property, he'll honor that."

"Don't be so sure. I like Jay, but he's a Wakefield. That's all I'm saying. They eat their biscuits cold. Somebody's got to get him to admit that his granddaddy was a

216

cheat and a liar. Tough job." She paused. "I think Gabby's perfect for it."

I was reduced to sputtering, "What, wait, wha, huh?" while the smell of trouble rose in my mind along with the thought of Gabby squaring off against Jay Wakefield. Trouble smells like burnt toast. I could make a lot of crispy croutons with this much scorched bread. "Gabby's not the diplomat of the family," I finally managed. "Not the negotiator, and definitely not the peace-maker. She says it's an accident that John Michael Michael got stabbed with a pickle fork, but he'd come straight from a movie set, and he was wearing some kind of full armor for the role, so I don't see how he could have sat down on the fork so that it just *happened* to stab him in the crack between the hip piece and the thigh sec-tion."

"Good aim?" Doug inserted drily.

"She did what?" Delta asked loudly. "She stabbed him in his crack? By lolly, I am pretty damn impressed!"

I groaned. "Have you got any advice for her? When I tell her what you've just told us, she may sharpen her pickle forks and head for Asheville."

"Good! I hope so. Just remind her of this old saw: You can catch more flies with honey than you can with vinegar. Change *flies* to *Wakefields.*"

Once again, voices erupted in the background. Delta yelled, "You get that face-scrubbing goop away from me. Sea salt and essence of what? If I want to rub my skin with salt, I'll go stand in a smokehouse and pretend I'm a side of bacon." To me she said, "Welcome home, Tal. Now get Gabby and Gus here, too. Y'all gotta take back what's yours. Bye, y'all!"

Click

She Responded with Relish

I typed on Doug's computer:

Dear Gabby,

Stop avoiding the phone. I know you really did stab JMM in the butt with that fork. I saw the report on E7. It's okay. Let me know the court date, and I'll be there. I just want to be sure that you're as calm as you say you are about the Wakefield situation and that you'll let me and Doug try to handle it. I keep getting the vinegar aroma, worse than before. Doug and I will meet with Jay in person the day after Christmas, we promise! Please call or text. Keep saying

to yourself, HONEY, NOT VINEGAR.
Please?

Love you,
Tal

Reading over my shoulder, Doug grunted.
"I swear I'm startin' to smell pickles, myself."

And They Heard Him Exclaim as He Drove Out of Sight

The biscuit witch, the Pickle Queen, and
the Kitchen Charmer. We're the soul-food-
surviving, finger-lickin'-good-at-heart,
handmade-from-scratch children of the best
cook in Asheville, North Carolina and the
bravest busboy/ex-army/police officer who
ever strapped on an apron in devotion to
his wife and kids. We are the MacBrides.
Our family tree sprouts buttered blossoms
with sweet-pickled berries. Our roots are
sunk deep in the Eternal Kitchen of the
Lard. We are Southern by birth, foodies at
heart, and world travelers by necessity.
Mama nicknamed us the Witch, the Queen,
and the Charmer with uncanny accuracy.
She saw our hidden ingredients.

Whatever happened next, whatever the
true story of Free Wheeler and its ties to
our family, I was home and happy.

And that's a start.

A Poem for the Season

The goat and our daughter were snug in
their bed
With visions of crayons alight in their
heads
The biscuits were cooling, and plenty to
spare
So Doug and I snuggled, with n'ary a care
He in his sweatpants, so threadbare,
appealing!
Me in a nightgown, some cleavage
revealing,
The fireplace crackled, the tree was
a-twinkle
The pigs were outside, enjoying a tinkle
When what to my wondering eyes should
appear
But a sweet diamond ring, suspended in
beer.
Out of the suds it flew with a splash.
I could tell from the carats, he'd invested
some cash
Doug's eyes, how they crinkled, his
proposal, so caring
Would I be his wife, for a life we'd be
sharing?
Of course I said yes, and we turned out the
light

Happy baking to all, and to all, a good
night.

Christmas Day

ALL OUT OF HONEY
IN ASHEVILLE WITH JAY
I LOVE HIM
PLEASE HELP
ABBY

ABOUT THE AUTHOR

Deborah Smith is the author of more than thirty-five novels in romance and women's fiction, including the *New York Times* best-seller, *A Place to Call Home*, and the *Wall Street Journal* bestseller, *The Crossroads Café*. She is also a founding partner and editorial director of Bell Bridge Books, a Memphis-based publishing company known for quality fiction and non-fiction by new and established authors. *The Biscuit Witch* is the first of THE CROSSROADS CAFÉ NOVELLAS, spin-offs set in the Appalachian world of *The Crossroads Café*.

Visit Deb at www.deborah-smith.com.

The employees of Thorndike Press hope you have enjoyed this Large Print book. All our Thorndike, Wheeler, and Kennebec Large Print titles are designed for easy reading, and all our books are made to last. Other Thorndike Press Large Print books are available at your library, through selected bookstores, or directly from us.

For information about titles, please call:
    (800) 223-1244

or visit our Web site at:
    http://gale.cengage.com/thorndike

To share your comments, please write:
    Publisher
    Thorndike Press
    10 Water St., Suite 310
    Waterville, ME 04901